O.M.G

OH MY GODMOTHER

THE MAGIC MISTAKE

O·M·G

OH MY GODMOTHER

★THE★
★MAGIC★
MISTAKE

By Barbara Brauner
and James Iver Mattson

Illustrated by
Abigail Halpin

Disney ★ HYPERION ★ Los Angeles ★ New York

SUSTAINABLE
FORESTRY
INITIATIVE

Certified Chain of Custody
Promoting Sustainable Forestry

www.sfiprogram.org
SFI-01054

The SFI label applies to the text stock

O.M.G

OH MY GODMOTHER

THE MAGIC MISTAKE

PROLOGUE

My name is Lacey Unger-Ware, and I *can't* make your dreams come true.

Most people wouldn't need to tell you that, but I do.

That's because, for a couple of weeks, I was a substitute fairy godmother. You wouldn't believe how hard it was—I almost got eaten by lions, and that was on a good day!

Now I'm out of the fairy-godmother business and happy to be an ordinary kid again.

"Ordinary" *rocks.*

CHAPTER 1

OMG! It's my wedding day!

I walk down the aisle in the most beautiful wedding dress you've ever seen: yards of billowing satin, a hundred pearl buttons down the back, and a train that goes on forever and ever.

The church is packed with people, and they all wipe tears from their eyes as the organist plays my favorite song, "I'm a Little Teapot."

Hmmm . . . "Little Teapot" isn't my favorite song, but I'm not going to let it ruin my special day.

When I reach the front of the church, my tall, handsome groom takes my hand. His golden eyes meet mine.

Golden eyes? That's strange. But not as strange as his spiky white whiskers. Or his long, sharp teeth. Or his horrible tuna breath.

We say our vows, and then the minister tells him, "You may kiss the bride!"

And Mr. Tuna Breath leans forward and sticks out his sandpapery tongue. Ewww!

I wake up with a shriek—and look into the golden eyes of my cat, Julius, who's sitting on my chest and meowing. I don't need to speak cat to know he's saying, "Feed me! Feed me NOW!"

My little sister, Madison, is out in the hallway singing "I'm a Little Teapot." It's *her* favorite song, and it's not fair that it got stuck in *my* dream.

I roll over and try to go back to sleep, but Mom pokes her head into the room and says, "Get up, Lacey. You don't want to be late for the wedding."

OMG! What if it wasn't a dream?

Then I remember. We're not going to my wedding (I'm twelve—give me a break!), we're going to Sunny's mom's wedding.

Sunny Varden is my best friend, and her mom—who everyone calls Gina, even me—is getting married for the second time at City Hall.

Sunny isn't sure how much she likes Gina's fiancé, Dwight. I'm not sure either—he treats me and Sunny like we're five. But I do have to say he's got beautiful white teeth. He should—Sunny says he's always at the dentist getting them cleaned.

When we get to City Hall, Sunny and Gina are already there.

Madison lets go of my hand and tugs on the sleeve of Gina's plain yellow dress. "Where's your wedding gown?"

Gina says, "This is it. Don't you like it?"

Madison makes the same face she does when Mom tries to make her eat broccoli. "No! And where are all the people?"

"It's just us," Gina says. "Dwight wanted things simple."

Madison *hates* simple. She tells Gina, "When I get married, it's going to be very, very fancy!"

I believe her. Madison's the only girl in kindergarten who wears a feather boa for juice break.

Madison looks at Gina suspiciously. "There's going to be a cake, right?"

"Yes! Seven-layer lemon cake with buttercream frosting!"

"And frosting flowers?"

"A whole garden of them."

Madison looks happy, but I notice that Mom and Dad keep glancing at the clock. I whisper to Sunny, "Where's Dwight?" Sunny just shrugs, and then she looks at the clock, too.

Gina's cell phone finally rings. "Dwight, honey, are you on your way?" I don't hear the answer, but Gina goes as white and still as a statue.

"Gina, what's wrong?" Mom asks.

Gina drops the phone like it's burning her hand, and Mom picks it up. "Dwight?"

As Mom listens, her jaw gets those lumps on either side of her face that mean she's really, really mad. She hangs up the phone. "Dwight's not coming. He just married his dental hygienist."

No wonder his teeth were so white!

Sunny puts her arms around Gina, and then we all do. But this isn't a happy hug, it's the saddest hug of all time.

Madison says, "Dental genies are evil!"

And she's completely, 100 percent right.

Gina pretty much stays in bed for the next month.

This is extra sad, because Gina is just like Sunny, only grown up. Gina's usually really energetic and happy—when there's a sleepover at Sunny's house, we have to beg her to stop giggling and let us go to sleep. Now all she *does* is sleep.

My mom sends over a lot of casseroles and soup, but Gina doesn't eat any of them. She only eats wedding cake. She tells Sunny that she paid seven hundred dollars for it and she's going to eat it all, even if it kills her.

I feel bad for Gina, and I feel worse for Sunny. Sunny's usually the happiest person I know, but it's hard to be happy when your mom's so miserable.

CHAPTER

2

Right now I wish *I* was home in bed eating wedding cake. Instead, at the end of a long day at school, I'm standing in gym class trying to make a free throw. And I really *am* trying.

I don't know why it's so hard for me. After all, my whole family is athletic: Dad played football in college, Mom runs marathons, and Madison's been dancing since she could walk.

I'm not a klutz, exactly. But I lack . . . *talent.* The only game I'm good at is Monopoly.

Since we started the basketball unit in PE, I've been practicing at home with Dad, and he says I'm getting better. I'm pretty sure he's lying, but maybe he's not, and maybe basketball is my sport.

Makayla, a cheerleader who hates me (long story), shouts, "Throw the stupid ball, Underwear Girl!"

So I throw the ball and hope for the best.

Instead of going in the basket, the ball hits Makayla on the head. "Ow! You did that on purpose!"

I can tell she's going to make a big deal about it, but then the bell rings and I make a dash for the door.

Mrs. Brinker, the PE teacher, stops me before I can leave. "Not so fast, Lacey. I won't have horseplay in my gym."

"But it was an accident! I couldn't hit Makayla on purpose in a million years!"

"And I won't have back talk! Run ten laps around the gym, *now*!"

Perfect ending to a perfect class. I do my ten laps and get hot, sweaty, and gross. Why does Mom like running? What is wrong with her?

I finally walk out the gym door, wiping my dripping face with my sleeve, and run right into Scott Dearden, my handsome boyfriend, who has the world's longest eyelashes.

Actually, he is handsome, but he's not my boyfriend. Last month Scott and I went to a football game together—almost a date! But his mom made him bring his three horrible little brothers, who kept singing "Scott and Lacey sitting in a tree, K-I-S-S-I-N-G!" Scott and I were so embarrassed that we've been avoiding each other ever since.

"Uh, hi, Lacey," Scott says.

"Uh, hi, Scott," I say, wishing I didn't look like I just ran ten laps. I desperately try to think of something cool to say. Something captivating and alluring.

There's a long pause.

Okay, I can't think of something captivating and alluring. I just need to think of anything. A few words I can make into a sentence.

"Scott! Are you here for basketball tryouts? I know you'll be great!" But it's not me who says that, it's Makayla, looking all made-up and not sweaty.

Scott smiles at her. "Thanks! Yeah, Coach Overdale says I have a pretty good chance of making the team."

Makayla says, "I'll be cheering for you!"

Scott and Makayla keep chatting like I'm not even there, so I slink away.

When I reach my locker, Sunny and Paige Harrington are waiting for me.

Remember how I said I used to be a fairy godmother? Well, Paige was my Cinderella, and I helped make her dream come true.

And since Sunny helped me help Paige, we're all friends now, which is amazing, because Paige is the most beautiful and popular girl in school and Sunny and I . . . aren't.

I'm about to start complaining about my cruddy day when I notice how depressed Sunny looks. It's so *not* like Sunny, at least not until the Dwight disaster. "You guys want to go to the mall?" I ask.

Sunny loves the mall. Even when she doesn't have any money, she can spend all afternoon just walking around.

But Sunny shakes her head. "I'd better see how my mom's doing."

Paige asks, "Should we make her some brownies? That always cheers people up."

Another head shake from Sunny. "It's wedding cake or nothing."

I close my locker, wishing I had something to say to make Sunny feel better. But I just don't.

Just then, Principal Nazarino passes us in the hall and we all shrink back a little. She's not mean, exactly, but she loves telling kids what to do. I guess that's why she became a principal. Today, though, she just smiles at us. "Sunny, are you ready for next Wednesday?"

"Next Wednesday?"

"For the mascot competition."

Sunny shakes her head no, and Principal Nazarino looks surprised.

Let me explain: our school teams used to be the Lincoln Railsplitters, and the mascot dressed up like Abraham Lincoln and carried a great big ax. (Because that's how rail-splitters split rails.) But when last year's Abraham Lincoln chopped the tail off the Wolverines' mascot, the school board said the ax had to go.

Abraham Lincoln *without* an ax is lame, so next Wednesday there's going to be a new mascot competition. Sunny signed up for it weeks ago; her idea was to call the team the Lincoln Labradoodles—labradoodles are her favorite kind of dog. But before she started making the costume, the wedding happened (or *didn't* happen).

The competition could be exactly what Sunny needs to cheer her up. So I say, "Sunny, I'll help you make the costume. It'll be fun!"

And Paige says, "I'll help you, too."

Sunny just shakes her head again and doesn't even wait for me and Paige as she walks down the hallway and out the door.

I look at Principal Nazarino. "Don't listen to Sunny. She's going to be in the competition, and she's going to win!"

Paige stares at me like I've gone crazy, but I still think this is just what Sunny needs.

Three hours later, I'm in the kitchen of my parents' restaurant, the Hungry Moose, and I'm putting the finishing touches on a labradoodle costume for Sunny. It's mainly made out of glued-together brown paper bags, but I think it's going to be cute in that silly, mascot kind of way.

As Mom and Madison watch, I put the brown paper head on Dad and stand back. "Ladies and gentlemen! Meet the new Lincoln Middle School mascot!"

Madison says, "Daddy looks like a big poop."

Mom puts her hand over Madison's mouth, but I see that she's trying not to smile herself. "Daddy does not look like a big poop. He's a moose, like our restaurant. Very cute, Lacey."

"He's not a moose. He's a dog."

Mom and Madison both tilt their heads, thinking about what I've just said.

Madison pulls Mom's hand off her mouth. "He's the ugliest dog I've ever seen."

Dad starts making barking sounds. "Woof! Woof! I'm an ugly, poopy dog!"

I know my feelings should be hurt, but I can't help laughing. When my family's right, they're right. But now what am I going to do?

CHAPTER 3

That night in my bedroom, I look for mascot costumes online. I've got about thirty dollars from birthday gift cards, which seems like a lot of money. But thirty dollars won't even pay for the shipping. Plus, there are no labradoodle costumes at all. Hardly anybody's even heard of a labradoodle.

You have, right? A labradoodle is a cross between a Labrador and a poodle. Everybody knows that, except for eight billion costume Web sites.

As I scroll through page after page of costumes, what I mainly see is vampires and zombies. As much as I want to do something for Sunny, all these zombies are creeping me out.

I almost jump out of my skin when there's a *tap-tap-tap* at the door. I get up to answer it, but no one's there—not even a zombie.

A moment after I sit back down, there's the same *tap-tap-tap*.

"That's not funny, Madison!" I call.

Tap-tap-tap.

I'm ready to rush to the door again—and then I realize the sound is coming from the curtain-covered window.

Now I'm *really* creeped out. I'm *this* close to crawling into bed and pulling the covers over my head. . . .

TAP-TAP-TAP-TAP-TAP.

What is making that noise? I have to know, so I fling open the curtains.

On the other side of the glass, a three-inch-tall fairy with beautiful butterfly wings glares at me. It's Katarina Sycorax, the crankiest fairy godmother you'd ever want to meet. When I was a substitute fairy godmother, Katarina was the fairy I was substituting for. But since that's been over for a while, I never thought I'd see her again.

"Katarina!" I say.

"Stop gawking and let me in!" she shouts, as loudly as a three-inch-tall fairy can. "Do you want me to tap all night?"

I push open the window, and she flutters in and lands on my dresser.

"What are you doing here?" I ask.

She takes her time fixing her wild, bright, red hair in the mirror. Then she finally turns to me with a bow, and, like she's working from a movie script, says, "Greetings and salutations! Before I can inform you of your great good fortune, please confirm that you are, indeed, one Lacey Unger-Ware."

"Of course I am. Why are you talking like that?"

"Don't interrupt! Confirm your name, or this is going to take all night."

"Yeah, I'm Lacey!"

"Do it right!"

Giving her a little bow that I hope looks sarcastic, I say, "Yes, I am indeed one Lacey Unger-Ware!"

Streamers and confetti fall from the ceiling like I've just won the big prize on a game show, and the light in the room changes from normal to glowing pink. Katarina gives herself another look in the mirror: "So flattering!"

I shake confetti out of my hair, really confused. Then I think

I know why Katarina's here. "Oh my gosh! Are you *my* fairy godmother? Are my dreams about to come true?"

My dreams flash through my mind. Dreams about rescuing endangered tigers. Dreams about running through swanky New York stores with armloads of the latest clothes. Dreams about actually making a basket in PE.

Katarina says, "No! This is an even greater honor!" She pauses dramatically.

The light in the room gets even pinker; my heart pounds in my chest.

"You, Lacey Unger-Ware, have been selected by the Godmothers' League to be a fairy-godmother-in-training!" Katarina waves her hand, and a tiny wand and a tiny envelope magically appear and float a couple of inches in front of my face. The envelope has a sparkly pink ribbon tied around it.

"What's in the envelope?" I ask, plucking it out of the air. Then I notice some teeny-tiny fine print on the outside: *Opening this envelope commits the recipient to the Godmothers' League Training Program. Warning! There is no going back!*

Wait a minute! With a sinking feeling, I carefully put the envelope down on the dresser and sit on the bed. The wand hovers near my head as I ask again, "What's in the envelope? And what does it mean there's no going back?"

Katarina ignores my questions and keeps speaking in the same movie-script way: "Before you can be admitted to the

Godmother Academy, there will be a test of your intelligence, skill, and natural ability. A client has been selected for you, and her name is in this envelope. You have between now and the precise moment of the next full moon to achieve her dream."

The envelope sparkles like it's saying, *Open me! Open me!* The wand does a little twirl and sparkles, too, then floats up to my face again. I swat at it. "Go away!"

Katarina says, "You don't understand what a rare privilege this is! The Academy accepts only a few girls a year. You'll have a full scholarship and be instructed, fed, clothed, and housed, all at the godmothers' expense."

All right, the Academy sounds kind of cool. It might even be fun. "So it's like a summer program?"

Katarina, happy to see that I'm finally a little interested, says, "It's exactly like a summer program! A fabulous summer boarding school that lasts a hundred years."

"A hundred years? That's a joke, right?"

"Godmothers rarely joke. Although I just heard this funny one where a fairy godmother, an elf, and a pixie walk into a bar and—"

"A HUNDRED YEARS! What about my family! What about my friends?"

"A small sacrifice! In ten years, you'll barely remember them."

"But I *want* to remember them!" I grab the wand and the envelope and shove them back at Katarina. "I won't do it!"

She doesn't take them. "You ingrate! You're actually saying no?"

"That's right! No, no, no! Also, no!"

The pink light fades from the room, and the magic streamers and confetti vanish.

Katarina angrily flutters her wings. "I never imagined you'd be this stupid! No one's turned us down in centuries—and Joan of Arc *regretted* it!" Katarina raises her pointy little chin. "So, that's your final answer?"

"Yes!" I try to hand the envelope and wand to her again. "You can take these with you! I don't want them!"

"They were made for you! They'll turn to dust when the moon is full."

"The wand isn't even my size! It's tiny!"

"When you get to the Academy, we shrink you down to match the wand."

"I DON'T WANT TO BE THREE INCHES TALL!"

Katarina gives me a look that says, *You are the stupidest girl in the world.* (It's quite a look.) Then she flies out the window into the night.

For a second I feel bad that Katarina's so upset. I thought we were kind of friends. But come on! I'm not going to leave my family! I can't believe she even suggested it.

The little wand and the envelope lie in my hands like they're daring me to use them. And I can still almost hear the envelope saying, *Open me! Open me!* I've got to get rid of them.

I rush into the bathroom to flush them down the toilet. But what if they clog it? And what if it's a magic clog that blows up the toilet and bursts all the pipes? I'd be grounded for . . . a hundred years.

I could throw the wand and the envelope into the trash, but Madison might see them and dig them out. A couple of zaps from her and we'd all be wearing tutus and living in a house made of Skittles.

So I go back into my bedroom and hide the wand and the sealed envelope on the highest shelf, behind my oldest stuffed animals.

Even Madison won't find them there.

CHAPTER 4

The next morning, I think I just dreamed that Katarina was here, so I climb on a chair and check; the little wand and envelope are still on the high shelf, right where I left them. I'll be glad when the full moon comes and I can sweep the two little piles of dust into the garbage can.

Over the next couple of days, I fuss some more with Sunny's mascot costume, but I finally give up. I'm just not crafty enough to make something that doesn't look like poop, and I'm not rich enough to buy anything. I'll need to think of something else to make Sunny happy.

On Saturday morning, I try to get Sunny to come with me to the petting zoo where I'm an intern. If bunnies and chicks don't make you happy, nothing will. But Sunny says she wants to see if she can get her mom out of bed and back to work in her art studio. (Gina has a cool job drawing the pictures for kids' books; she even volunteers with the art program at Lincoln.)

So I'm all by myself as usual when I arrive at the petting zoo. The animals are superhappy to see me, and I stop worrying and smile. This really is the best job ever. Everybody's hungry, and I run around opening feed bins and scooping out food.

"Stop that, you little brats!"

Huh? I turn around and see Scott on the other side of the petting-zoo gate taking a basketball away from his three demonic little brothers. He tells them, "Don't throw the ball at the meerkats!"

"Hi, Scott!" I call.

Scott smiles at me—and his brothers use it as an opportunity to run whooping down the hill out of sight. Scott sighs.

"Aren't you going to go get them?" I ask.

"They'll be fine. They don't listen to me anyway." He dribbles the ball. "Did you hear I made the basketball team?"

"That's great!"

"Coach Overdale says I'm supposed to eat, drink, and sleep with this basketball." Then Scott says, "Think fast!"

He tosses the ball at me and, not expecting it, I gawk like a dork and let it bounce away. The ball lands between Lewis and Clark, the goats, who try to eat it.

I say, "And *that* is why I'm going to flunk gym."

"You're not going to flunk gym." Scott climbs over the gate and points at a feed bin. "Pick up the ball and toss it in, nice and easy."

There's nothing easy about this, but I fling the ball anyway.

"Ow!" Scott yelps. If you got points for hitting people on the head, I'd be a star.

"Sorry." I give the ball back to Scott. "I'm the worst."

"No, you're not. The problem's with your follow-through. Let me show you." He holds up the ball, looking like a basketball star. He shoots . . .

. . . and misses the bin by a mile. Scott turns red.

Curly, the sheep, *baas*, and I swear it sounds like he's laughing.

The basketball rolls over to Gus, the pony, who gives it a swift kick with a hind leg. The ball whooshes into the feed bin without even touching the sides.

Scott whistles, impressed. "Nothing but net. Forget about me—you should let the pony coach you."

I laugh. Somehow, Scott's *not* being perfect at everything makes me like him even more.

Then Raymond, who's in charge of the petting zoo, walks in, dripping wet.

"What happened to you?" I ask.

"Three crazy little boys jumped into the flamingo pond. I can't catch them, so I'm calling the guards."

Scott turns pale. "Gotta go!"

He grabs the basketball, jumps over the gate, and sprints down the hill toward the pond.

In the afternoon, I knock on Sunny's front door. Every month there's a group demonstration in her karate class, and I always go with her and her mom.

While I'm waiting for Sunny to let me in, Fifi, the poodle who lives next door, barks at me. She's got one of those fussy poodle haircuts, and pink bows on her ears. I wonder if dogs can be embarrassed.

The door finally opens, and Sunny comes outside, already dressed in her white karate uniform. She hands me a camera. "My mom wants you to take pictures."

"Isn't she coming?"

"No."

I'm shocked. Sunny's mom has never, ever, missed a monthly demo. "*Why* isn't she coming?"

"'Cause she wants to sit in her bathrobe, eat wedding cake, and watch the *Bridemonsters* marathon on cable." (*Bridemonsters* is this show where women go berserk when they get married.)

I say, "Your mom's not getting any less sad, is she?"

"No."

"Did you at least get her into her art studio?"

"No."

"What are you going to do?"

"There's nothing I can do."

"But she can't stay in her bathrobe forever!"

Sunny picks at the paint on the porch rail. "I'm not so sure."

Sunny and I hardly say another word on the long, long walk to karate class.

CHAPTER

5

Usually after karate class, Gina takes me and Sunny out for burgers. But tonight, since we're Gina-less, Sunny just goes home and so do I.

Mom, Dad, and Madison are at the restaurant, and the house is quiet and empty when I walk in.

I go to my room—and I find that the stuffed animals from the top shelf have been knocked down onto the bed. What the heck happened?

Then I see an orange tail wagging in the middle of the pile of stuffed animals. It's Julius!

"Bad kitty! What were you doing up on that shelf?"

I pull away four stuffed bears, one stuffed shark, and three stuffed elephants, finally uncovering one live cat. He's got a pink ribbon in his mouth. A pink ribbon that is tied to . . .

. . . the magic envelope!

Oh no.

Oh no!

OH NO!

Without even thinking about it, I grab the envelope away from him. The pink ribbon slides out from the bow, the bow comes apart, and the flap pops open. All at once, streamers and confetti fall from the ceiling, and the room is filled with that annoying pink light again. And this time, trumpets sound. (I'm so glad Mom and Dad aren't home!)

Julius, not a trumpet fan, yowls and scrambles out of the room.

I desperately try to retie the envelope, but the flap won't stay closed. So I do the only thing I can think of—I sit on it. But the confetti just keeps falling, and the trumpets keep blaring.

A moment later, Katarina taps at the window. Without getting up from the bed, I reluctantly reach over and let her in. She flies up to me, smiling and happy.

Maybe if I pretend that I have no idea what's going on, Katarina will leave and I can put the envelope in Mom's shredder. So I say, all innocent, "Hey, there! What a nice surprise!"

"You opened the envelope!"

"No, I didn't!"

"I see confetti and streamers."

"Birthday party."

"I hear trumpets."

"My neighbor's in a band."

"And you're sitting on something!"

"Just my bed. Comfy!"

Katarina glares at me and pulls out her wand. "So if I do a spell that burns up the envelope I gave you, you won't mind?"

"Why would I mind?"

Katarina raises her wand and chants, "If Lacey's a liar, her pants catch on fire."

She looks likes she means business, so I yell, "STOP!"

Katarina flicks her wand anyway, and I cringe, but all she's doing is turning off the music. The silence in the room is somehow even louder than the trumpets were.

I guiltily slide the envelope out from under me and put it on the bed. "Okay, okay! It's open. But it's Julius's fault!"

Katarina rolls her eyes. "Why am I not surprised? I hate that miserable furbag."

"So it doesn't count that it's open, right?"

"Of course it counts! You can't reseal an envelope."

"Sure you can! I've got glue, Scotch tape, or stickers. Take your pick."

"You can't reseal a *magic* envelope. Whether the cat made you do it or not, the test began the second you pulled that ribbon. You have between now and 9:23 on Friday night to make your client's dreams come true."

"Why 9:23?"

"That's the precise time that the moon is full this month. People always think it's right at midnight, but it can be any time. 4:10 in the morning. 1:50 in the afternoon. This month, it's Friday at 9:23 p.m. A mere six days from now!"

"This is crazy! I don't want to be a fairy godmother! And I won't do the test!"

"All right, don't. Then you'll fail. But I warn you, if you fail—"

I know this is going to be bad. Fairies look all sweet and nice, but they play rough.

"—you'll never find comfortable shoes again in your entire life."

I blink at Katarina, surprised. "I can live with that."

"Also, your client will be unhappy for the rest of her life."

I don't want to be mean, but it's either her or me. "I can live with that."

"Also, in addition to the shoes and the unhappy client . . . If you fail, people will hate you. Every single human being in the world will shudder at the very sight of you."

Okay, I *can't* live with that. I say, "That doesn't even make sense! Why would people hate me?"

"People love you when you make their dreams come true. The hating comes when you ruin their dreams. And it's not only hating, it's also spitting and hair-pulling."

The last time I got tangled up with Katarina, there were a couple of weeks when every animal on earth hated my guts, and that was awful. It would be way worse if every person on earth hated me.

I say in a trembling voice, "So there's no way I can win. If I fail the test, people hate me. And if I pass, I get sent away to godmother school for a hundred years." I can't help it; I start to cry.

Katarina flies onto my shoulder and pats it. "Don't take it so hard. Someone very wise once said there's no situation so bad there isn't a little good in it. Who said that? Oh! I think it was me."

"There's nothing good in this." I keep crying.

Katarina stops patting my shoulder—she's not too great with sympathy. "Snap out of it, Lacey! You only have six days. You need to see who your client is and get started."

When I keep crying and ignoring her, Katarina aims her wand at the envelope, and it floats up in front of my eyes. A cream-colored card slides out, full of tooth marks from where Julius has chewed on it. But the words are still readable: *Your client is Gina, who wants a dream wedding to her true love.*

Shocked, I stop crying and stare at the card. "Gina? That's Sunny's mom! But I can't help her. Her true love is already married to a dental hygienist."

"Then he's not her true love. And that's the last hint I can give you. From this point forward, I'm here only to observe your progress, and I can't give you any help or advice. Ask me no questions."

Katarina waves her wand and there's a buzzing mosquito noise, but I don't see anything. Then she says, in a very serious tone, "I've released the pinch gnats."

I have no idea what she's talking about. "What's a pinch gnat?" I ask. Then—*ow!* Something pinches me on the arm, really hard.

Katarina says grandly, "I can help you no more!"

"So they're going to be here the whole time?" Ow! Something pinches me on my elbow. "Was that a pinch gnat?" OW!! Something pinches my other elbow. "How do I make them stop?" OW! OW! OW! I get pinched all over.

Katarina says, "The pinch gnats are here to make sure you don't ask me any questions."

Like I said, fairies play rough.

The pinching stops and I look at my arms, expecting to see welts all over them. But invisible gnats leave invisible marks.

So, whether I want to be or not, I'm back in the fairy-godmother business. And maybe I *can* make some good come out of a bad situation. There may not be a happy ending for me, but at least I can make sure that Gina and Sunny have one.

I dig through the stuffed animals on my bed and find the little wand. I pick it up and feel a small zap of electricity going up my arm, and the tip of the wand glows bright.

I, Lacey Unger-Ware, am now officially a Godmother Academy candidate.

Yikes.

I'm going to need some backup. I need a godmother posse. So I text Sunny and Paige: *EMERGENCY! MEET ME TOMORROW AT FOUNTAIN PARK, 8 A.M.!!!!!!!!!!!!!!!!!!*

Katarina pulls out a little notebook and starts writing in it—about me, I bet. It makes me really, really nervous, so I send one more text: *!!!*

CHAPTER 6

When I reach the park a little before eight the next morning, Sunny and Paige are already sitting in the fountain. That would be a problem if the fountain worked, but it's been dry for as long as I can remember. Nobody comes to this park anymore, so I thought it would be the perfect place to meet and talk.

"What's going on?" Paige asks.

Before I have a chance to say anything, Katarina flies out of my pocket and waves. "Hiya, girls."

"Katarina! You're back!" Paige says, jumping up.

Sunny looks happier than I've seen her since her mom didn't-get-married. (It's so great to see a big smile back on her face.) She climbs out of the fountain and holds out her arms to give Katarina a hug, which is not easy when the hug-ee is three inches tall. So Sunny finally says, "Big hug!" and forms a circle with her arms around Katarina's airspace.

I know that Sunny and Paige must be wondering what's going on, so I quickly say, "Don't ask Katarina any questions! There are pinch gnats!"

Sunny turns to me. "Can we ask *you* questions?"

Without even thinking, I ask Katarina, "They can ask me questions, right?" Then, OW! I get pinched on both sides of my face. Katarina smirks and scribbles something in her notebook.

Paige cocks an eyebrow. "So, what's a pinch gnat?"

Sunny says, "And are you a fairy godmother again?"

I pause to see if the gnats are going to pinch *them* for asking questions. When nothing happens, I quickly tell Paige and Sunny why Katarina's come back, leaving out the part about being sent

away to school for a hundred years. (They'd freak out. I know it.) I skip straight to the reason I need their help: "Between now and Friday, I have to make somebody's dream come true."

Sunny says, *"Who is it?"*

"It's . . . Gina."

Paige looks confused. "Gina who? There's no Gina at our school."

Sunny says, "The only Gina I know is . . ." Then she starts jumping up and down. "OMG! OMG! It's my mom! It's my mom! That's so great!"

Paige says, "But she's old." Sunny gives her a dirty look.

I say, "She's not old. And even if she is, old people can have dreams, too."

Katarina snorts, but since I can't ask her whether she's snorting about dreams or old people, I ignore her and turn to Sunny. "Your mom's dream is getting married to her true love. And I have to make it happen by Friday night."

Sunny looks confused. "Her 'true love'? Who is that?"

"That's the hard part. I don't know."

Paige shakes her head and whistles. "And you thought it was tough being *my* fairy godmother!"

Sunny looks at me, shocked. "You don't know? You're just going to find her some guy?"

I say, "He won't be some guy, he'll be her true love. And they'll live happily ever after."

"No, no, NO!"

"But—"

"No buts!" Sunny says. "Mom thought Dwight was her true love, and look what happened! She's still in her pajamas, eating wedding cake out of the freezer!"

"That's why she needs a fairy godmother! Katarina says if I don't do this for your mom, she'll be miserable for the rest of her life. You don't want that, do you?"

When Sunny just frowns, Paige steps out of the fountain and puts her arm around her. "Lacey did an awesome job when she was *my* fairy godmother."

Trying to decide what to do, Sunny looks over at Katarina to see what she thinks.

Katarina plasters on a blank expression and says in a flat voice, "I am only here as a neutral observer. I cannot insert my opinion into the proceedings in any way." But then she pretends to cough, and in between coughs she says, "Cough—DO IT!—cough!"

An instant later, Katarina shrieks and slaps the side of her neck—one of the invisible pinch gnats must have just gotten her. She yells at it: "I wasn't helping! I was coughing!"

I guess I'm not the only one the pinch gnats are keeping an eye on.

But Sunny must have heard the "DO IT," because she turns to me and says, "I don't want my mom to be miserable."

"So you'll help?"

"Yes! What do we need to do?"

I'm so happy I give Sunny a big hug. "The first thing we have to do is tell your mom I'm her fairy godmother. We can't do this without her."

Sunny leaps up and starts walking in the direction of her house. "Let's go!"

I say, "Sunny, hold up! What if she doesn't believe me?"

Sunny stops. "Of course she'll believe you."

Paige shakes her head. "Don't be so sure. It even took *me* a while to believe Lacey."

I say, "More than a while. You told me I was crazy."

"Because you did it all wrong. You can't just tell somebody you're a fairy godmother."

"So what am I supposed to do? Float up to her in a bubble like Glinda the Good Witch?"

Sunny asks, "Can you do that?"

CHAPTER

7

Half an hour later, I'm on my way to Sunny's house, floating high above Pine Street—in a pink bubble. This is so cool! Katarina peers out of my pocket unhappily, but I'm not going to let her rain on my parade.

The last time I worked with Katarina, I did a lot of practicing with a magic wand, so by now I'm pretty good at spells. It's all in the wrist. You can't just wave the wand, you have to say the spell out loud and toss it. Plus, the spell has to rhyme—that's the rule. I don't know *why* it's the rule, but it is.

To make this pink bubble, I chanted: "Convincing's no trouble when you ride in a bubble," flicked the wand, and tossed the spell at myself. So here I am!

The plan is for me to float in through Gina's bedroom window, bubble-style, and say, "Ta-da! I'm your fairy godmother! You're the lucky winner of a dream wedding!" Then Gina will light up like a Christmas tree and say, "Wow!" At least, I hope she will.

Sunny and Paige have already gone on ahead to make sure that the bedroom window's open and that Gina isn't in the bathroom. (That would be embarrassing for everybody.) So I'm pretty sure we've thought of everything.

The view is so beautiful up here in the bubble that it takes my breath away. It's like looking down at a living map, with trees and houses and streets stretching away in every direction. I turn around and try to find my house. There it is! It looks so—

"LOBSTER!" Katarina flies out of my pocket, shrieking— and slaps away an invisible pinch gnat on her neck. Does that mean she's helping me?

Yes, she's helping me, because when I turn back around, I see we're about to crash into a billboard for Lobster Shack. Plywood claws are inches away from bursting my bubble.

I've just discovered the problem with traveling this way: no brakes. Also—no steering wheel! And also—no air bags!

I scream and slam myself against the bottom of the bubble, and at the last possible moment, we dip under the billboard and pop up on the other side . . .

. . . where there are about a million pine trees. (Now I know where the street got its name.)

"TREES!" Katarina shouts; this is followed by "Ow! Ow! Ow!" She must be getting pinched all over by the invisible gnats.

I hurl myself back and forth against the sides of the bubble and finally manage to wobble us through the miniforest and out the other side.

What with Katarina screaming and me sweating buckets, the inside surface of the bubble is fogging up like a car window. My hand makes squeaky sounds as I try to wipe away the moisture. Through the clear spot, I see that we're almost at Sunny's house. I'm just glad she doesn't live on Pine Street.

Oh, geez.

Sunny doesn't live on Pine Street; she lives on Oak Street. I don't want to tell Katarina this—but I don't have to:

"OAK TREES! OAK TREES!" Katarina shouts; she follows up with more *ow-ow-ows*!

Oak trees with twisty, gnarled branches line both sides of Sunny's street.

And the biggest, twistiest oak tree of all is right outside Gina's second-floor window. The bubble heads straight for the tree. I've got to steer around it!

Too late.

pop

With that quiet little sound, the pink walls of the bubble burst into mist, leaving Katarina and me standing on nothing but air outside Gina's window. Katarina's fine—she's got wings. But I don't.

I scream as I nose-dive toward the ground. Then, with a

jolt, I stop in midair, right outside Gina's open bedroom window. What just happened?

Katarina hovers nearby, scribbling furiously in her notebook as I dangle like a puppet on a string.

I finally figure out that a big tree branch has snagged the back of my sweater. I reach behind me to grab the branch, but it's like trying to scratch the spot between your shoulder blades that you can never reach by yourself.

"Lacey! What are you doing?" Gina stands at the window wearing her broken-heart bathrobe and looking astonished.

I flash her my biggest, most fairy-godmother-like smile. "Ta-da!" I say.

Then: *crack!* The branch starts to break and I'm a second away from falling to the hard brick patio beneath me.

When there's another *crack*, Gina lunges halfway out the window to grab my arms as the big branch falls with an explosion of leaves, almost taking me down, too.

Gina's arms shake as she tries to pull me inside. But she's not strong enough—we're both going to fall.

Sunny and Paige suddenly poke their heads out of the window on either side of Gina. "Hang on!" Sunny yells.

"I'm trying! Help us!"

The girls reach out the window and, grabbing wrists and arms and anything else they can hold on to, finally haul Gina and me inside.

CHAPTER 8

It's exhausting when you almost get killed!

While Katarina floats above Gina's head, where Gina can't see her, the rest of us sit on the bedroom floor, panting.

Gina finally catches her breath enough to say, "Lacey! Why were you in that tree?"

Okay, so I messed up my big entrance, but maybe I can still make this work. I spread my arms dramatically and tell Gina, "I'm your fairy godmother! You're the lucky winner of a dream wedding!"

Gina just looks confused and says, "No, really. What were you doing in that tree?"

"I told you! I'm your fairy godmother, and I can do magic! It's going to be a lot of work, but by Friday night we're going to find you a new husband and throw you the fanciest wedding ever!"

Gina gives me a big hug. "Aren't you a sweetie! I wish you could do that, too."

She doesn't believe a single word I've just said. Thinking that maybe some magic will convince her, I reach into my pocket for the wand and say, "I'm not a sweetie, I'm a fairy godmother. Let me show you!" But the wand's not there—it must have fallen out when I was in the tree.

"Show me what?" Gina says.

I look at Katarina fluttering over Gina's head and get an idea. "There's another fairy in the room. Look above you!"

Gina looks up—but Katarina zips out of sight behind a lamp before Gina sees even a flash of butterfly wings.

Ow!!! The invisible pinch gnats attack me from all sides. I guess using Katarina for show-and-tell is cheating.

Gina looks at Paige, Sunny, and me with a sad smile. "I'm so glad you girls aren't too old to play fairy godmother. Stay kids as long as you can." She kisses us all on the forehead, then says, "There's another *Bridemonsters* marathon on TV. Anybody want to watch it with me?"

If you're ever a fairy godmother, remember: *no one* says "Wow," and lights up like a Christmas tree when you try to tell them who you are.

After a lot of searching, we finally find the wand. It's underneath the broken tree branch in a puddle of red sugar water from a tipped-over hummingbird feeder. As I wipe the wand clean, a few drops splash on Katarina.

"Be careful," she snaps.

"It's just sugar water," I tell her.

Sunny asks me, "Are you going to go up and talk to my mom some more?"

"No. Before I try again, we need a new plan."

"Like what?" Paige asks.

"That's what we need to figure out."

All of us flop down on the grass to think. The backyard is really quiet—there's just the faint sound of the *Bridemonsters* marathon and a slurping noise.

Slurping?

I look over and see Katarina drinking from the puddle of red hummingbird water like it's the best thing she ever tasted.

"Katarina! Gross!" I say. She ignores me, so I try not to watch.

Five minutes of hard thinking go by, and I ask the girls, "Anyone come up with a plan yet?"

Paige shakes her head. "Gina is never, ever going to believe you're her fairy godmother. You saw the way she looked at you— like you were a silly little kid."

Sunny nods, depressed. "She'll never get her dream wedding with her true love."

I tell the girls, "We can't give up. If Gina's not going to

believe me, I'm just going to have to give her a dream wedding without her help."

Paige says, "You can't have a wedding without a bride."

"There'll be a bride. By Friday, she'll want to get married for sure."

Sunny and Paige both ask, "Why?"

I can't think of a single good reason, but I still say, "Trust me. I'll figure this out."

Sunny and Paige don't look convinced. So I'm glad for the interruption when *BZZZ!!!!!* Katarina circles around the yard like a drunken bee.

BZZZZ!!! She circles a second time.

BZZZZ!!! BZZZZ!!! And a third and a fourth.

BZZZZZZZ!!!!! Katarina starts one more loop—and suddenly drops to the grass like a rock. We all gasp.

"What's wrong with her?" Sunny asks.

When I pick Katarina up, she's sticky and sound asleep. I tell the girls, "It's got to be a sugar crash. It happens to Madison whenever Grandma visits."

Katarina snores and smacks her sugar-sticky lips.

"She needs a nap. I'll text you guys later."

I'm glad to have an excuse to go. I need more time to think.

CHAPTER 9

When I get home, I put Katarina in the jewelry box on my dresser. She's still sleeping, and if she's at all like Madison, the sugar crash will zonk her out for another couple hours. And, just like Madison, Katarina looks so angelic and sweet—

"YOU IDIOT!" Katarina sits bolt upright in the jewelry box and shakes her fist at me. "That bubble trick was the stupidest thing you ever tried! And I don't know who that Glinda is, but she's an even bigger idiot than you are!"

"The bubble wasn't as stupid as you drinking all the hummingbird food!"

"I did not." Katarina burps loudly and looks a tiny bit embarrassed. She throws her hands up in the air in defeat. "And I was doing so well on my diet! But the pinch gnats drank more than I did."

"Pinch gnats like sugar water, too?" Oops—that question is

going to get me pinched for sure. I brace myself, waiting for an invisible attack. But nothing happens. "I didn't get pinched. Why not?" Double oops—that was another question. *Still* nothing.

Katarina calls, "Here, pinch gnats! Here, pinch gnats! Come here, you horrible creatures!"

When we don't hear a single angry buzz, Katarina looks at me and laughs. "I bet the greedy things never left the puddle."

"Really?"

"The only thing pinch gnats like more than pinching people is sugar water."

"How long before they come back?"

"Soon."

But they're not here right now. So this may be my chance to get some advice—if only Katarina will help. "Before they get back . . . can you help me with Gina's wedding?"

Katarina crosses her arms and stares at me. She's not saying yes, but she's not saying no.

"Katarina, if I can't get Gina married, every person in the world will hate me. I thought you were my friend. Can't you give me some help? Please! Just a little."

"I can't . . ."

My heart sinks.

". . . officially help you. *Unofficially*—well, you don't have a ghost of a chance without me. And, though you definitely have many flaws, you're not the worst girl in the world. I'm walking a very fine line, but I'll give you as many hints as I can. What do you want to know?"

I'm so happy I feel like hugging her. "I want to know everything! How do I get Gina married? Where do I find a guy?"

"Not just a guy, her true love!"

"Is there a spell I can use? A love spell?"

"Love spells don't last. This needs to be the real thing."

"But how will I *know*?"

"Relax. It's very simple. All you have to do is—OW!"

"All I have to do is 'OW'? What are you talking about?" Then I get pinched all over. I look down and see an ugly red bug, about the size of a bumblebee, on my arm. I shudder and flick it away.

There have got to be a dozen of these red bugs flying around Katarina and me. If they're pinch gnats, why aren't they invisible? And gnats are supposed to be tiny! These are *huuuuuuge*! One of them burps loudly, and I suddenly figure out what's going on: the gnats are big and red because they're full of red hummingbird food. Gross!

Dad suddenly calls from outside. "Lacey! You want to play some hoops?" I walk toward the window, and all the red bugs zip after me. Geez—I hope Dad can't see them from the driveway.

I call back: "I'm busy right now!"

"Don't you have gym tomorrow? You need the practice."

"Maybe later!"

I turn back to Katarina. "How am I going to explain big red

bugs to Dad and Mom?" I ask—and then get pinched on all sides. This is so annoying!

Since the pinch gnats are here again, Katarina can't help me, but there must be something *I* can do. After all, I'm smarter than a bunch of bugs, or at least I hope I am.

I know! *I* know!

I drag the vacuum cleaner in from the hall closet and plug it in.

"Lacey! Don't do that!" Katarina gives me a frightened look. She flies into my jewelry box and closes the lid.

Ignoring her, I turn the vacuum on. It only takes me a couple of seconds to suck up every pinch gnat in the room. "Katarina, you can come out, now. The problem's solved!"

Only it's not.

The vacuum cleaner buzzes and shakes as the angry pinch gnats try to get out, and then it slowly floats up above the ground—and lunges for my head!

I duck, and the vacuum smashes against the wall. Still floating, it spins around and lunges again. Screaming, I run out of the room with the vacuum cleaner following me, but then the vacuum stops with a jerk. It's reached the end of its cord.

If I were Madison, this is where I'd tell it, "Nyah-nyah-nyah." But I'm too mature for that. Oh, what the heck—I stick out my tongue and say, "Nyah-nyah-nyah."

The vacuum lunges at me like a pit bull on a chain—and yanks the cord out of the wall.

Eek!

It chases me down the hall, through the family room, around the dining room (where I circle the table three times), and finally into the kitchen.

I dash for the back door—and the vacuum smashes into it before I can turn the doorknob. The vacuum's lid pops off, and a dozen furious (and dusty!) pinch gnats burst out.

They corner me near the refrigerator. Ow! Ow! Ow! Ow! I get pinched all over. Where's a hummingbird feeder when I need one? Forget the feeder—I just need the sugar water.

Sugar water . . . that's like soda, right?

I fling open the refrigerator. Oh, no! There's not a bottle of soda in sight.

And then I see a little bit of red behind the cottage cheese and the Tupperware containers. I pull out a bottle of strawberry Fanta left over from when my aunt Ginny visited. (It's her favorite.)

There's a little hiss when I open the bottle, and the pinch gnats stop what they're doing and look at the bottle curiously. I think they can already smell the sugar.

I take a saucer out of the cupboard, and I'm about to fill it with soda, but then I stop. I don't want Mom and Dad to find a saucer full of bugs on the counter.

So I wave the bottle and lead the swarm back to my room like the Pied Piper, if the Pied Piper had used strawberry Fanta instead of a flute.

I put the saucer down on my dresser and pour out some of the soda. SLURP!!! The gnats attack it from all sides. Please, let this work!

Half an hour later, Katarina and I watch twelve huge red pinch gnats still slurping Fanta out of the nearly empty dish. They're yawning, and one by one they all clunk over, sound asleep. "Sugar crash?" I say.

Katarina nods.

"I like the pinch gnats a lot better when they're asleep."

"*Everybody* likes pinch gnats better when they're asleep."

"How long are they going to stay red? I can't walk around

all week with a swarm of big red bugs following me! I'd go from being Underwear Girl to Bug Girl."

"Relax. They'll digest the red overnight, and then they'll be invisible again."

"You're sure?"

"Have I ever been wrong before?"

I'm pretty sure she has, but now's no time for an argument. I just hope she's right. I say, "While they're sleeping, can I ask you something?"

Katarina nods.

"Before the pinch gnats came, you said, 'All you have to do is . . .' What were you going to say?"

"I was *going* to say, 'All you have to do is find her prince.'"

"*That's* your big advice? You do know there aren't a lot of princes around here, right?"

"Nonsense! There are princes all over the place."

I've never seen even one, but I hope she's right.

CHAPTER 10

Ow! Ow! Ow!

At the crack of dawn the next morning, I feel a dozen pinches.

OW! I sit up, and in the dim light from the window, I see that I'm covered with crawling bugs. The red color has faded almost entirely, but I can still make out their ghostly outlines.

Why are they pinching me? Was I asking questions in my sleep?

I shake them off my arms. Some of them land right back on me, pinching like crazy, while the others fly over to the half-full bottle of Fanta. They try to crawl inside, but they've grown too big to fit through the opening. They buzz around it unhappily and then zip back to me.

"Katarina! Wake up!" I say.

A moment later, the jewelry box lid pops open and Katarina peers out sleepily.

I point at the gnats. "They're almost invisible again—but they won't stop pinching! And I'm not even asking questions!"

Katarina watches the gnats as they take turns pinching me and then zooming back to the Fanta bottle. "For the love of glitter, pour them some soda!"

I hop out of bed—Ow! Ow! Ow!—and fill the empty saucer. The gnats forget me and surround the saucer like kittens lapping milk (mean, ugly, kittens). They almost instantly turn bright red again. We're back where we started—maybe even worse, because the gnats are bigger.

Katarina turns to me. "Well, I hope you're happy. You've turned them into sugar fiends."

"At least they've stopped pinching me," I say. I stare at the gnats, trying to figure out what to do next. I *really* can't have them following me around at school. Finally I say, "I know what I can do. I'll just fill up a huge bowl with soda—gallons and gallons— and they'll be so busy drinking they won't even think about me."

"Won't work. They'll drink till they explode. Trust me, pinch gnat guts are very hard to clean up. And the smell!"

"*Ew!* But if I just give them a little soda, they'll drink it all and come find me at school, for sure. I can't spend all week in my room making sure their dish is full!" Suddenly, I think of something. "But Katarina, *you* could."

"I'm not a waitress."

"No, you're a wonderful, generous, sweet fairy godmother who helps her friends. Please! It'll be like a vacation. All you have to do is sit here and trickle out a little soda once in a while."

"No."

"Please. Please. Pretty please. Please. Please. Please. *Pleeeeeeeease!*"

"All right! All right! I'll do it if you'll just shut up!" Katarina sighs. "I'm one of the greatest fairy godmothers in the country. No—why be modest? In the entire world! And I'm reduced to spending my time pouring out soda for bugs."

"I owe you."

"You're darn tootin' you do."

"And one more teeny little thing . . ."

Katarina raises an eyebrow.

"If it's okay with you, we need to move the saucer into the back of the closet so Mom won't see it."

Katarina looks toward the ceiling. "What, oh, what, did I do to deserve this?"

I guess that means yes.

When I get to school, Sunny sits down next to me in homeroom and says, "You didn't text me about how we're getting my mom married by Friday."

"I'm sorry! I got distracted because Katarina and I had a bug problem."

And for the rest of homeroom, Sunny and I talk about pinch gnats and about how Katarina's going to stay in my closet and feed them soda. As we leave the room, Sunny says, "We never talked about the wedding."

This was on purpose, since there's not much to talk about so far. "I'll give you all the details at lunch, okay?"

Sunny smiles—she completely trusts me.

By lunchtime, I need to have everything worked out. I'm sure I'll come up with something in English, World Cultures, or science.

I don't.

At lunchtime, I find Paige and Sunny in the cafeteria going through an old-style photo album. "What's that?" I ask.

Paige says, "It's from my mom and dad's wedding. I thought it might give us some ideas."

"Good thinking." I sit down next to them and look at a sweet picture of Paige's parents. It's a "walk down the aisle" shot taken a moment after the wedding ceremony, and they both look so happy they could burst.

I haven't seen that many pictures of Paige's mom, who died

before Paige and her dad moved here. I look at her mom's smiling face.

"She was so pretty," I tell Paige.

"Even your dad was pretty back then," Sunny says.

Paige points at her father's big grin. "Dad says it was the second-happiest day of his life."

"What was the happiest?" I ask.

"When I was born."

Sunny laughs. "That's what my mom says about me!"

I turn the album page, and there's a photo of Paige's mom throwing the wedding bouquet. Paige studies the picture, a little sad. I wonder if Paige will ever stop missing her. I know I'd never stop missing my mom if she died, so the answer must be no. But maybe after a while you remember the good times and think less about the sad ones.

We keep flipping through the album, and I open my notebook to make a list of all the things we need. "We've got to have a church. A minister. Flowers. A cake. And a beautiful, beautiful dress. Anything else?"

Sunny says, "Just one thing."

"Rice to throw?"

"Not rice. Lacey—where are we going to get a groom?"

Sunny and Paige look at me as if they expect me to know the answer. Like I'm a fairy godmother or something.

Oh, right. I am. All I can say is, "I'm still working on it!"

In PE, I'm extra sucky at basketball, because I'm trying to think of somebody for Gina to marry. The guy needs to be nice. He needs to really like kids, because Sunny is part of the package. He needs to be handsome, at least to Gina. And he needs to be able to come to a wedding on Friday. *His* wedding.

Mrs. Brinker blows her whistle right in my ear, and I jump about ten feet. "Lacey! You're not even pretending to focus!"

"Yes, I am. I'm very focused." Which is true—only, not on basketball.

"Everyone else is getting better, but you're getting worse. I want you to stay after school every day this week for remedial practice."

Makayla smirks at me. (Now I'm kind of glad that I hit her on the head with the basketball last week.)

But I don't have time for Makayla—or for remedial practice. I've got a wedding to plan and a lot of magic to do. Then I get an idea. I tell Mrs. Brinker, "Excuse me a second! I'll be right back!"

And with Mrs. Brinker and the kids all staring at me, I run toward the locker room. Mrs. Brinker shouts, "Lacey! You get back here this instant!" I pretend not to hear her.

In the locker room, I take the wand out of my sweater pocket. I need a spell! It's not helping that Mrs. Brinker is shouting through the door: "LACEY UNGER-WARE! If you're not back here by the time I count to ten, you're getting detention! One, two . . ."

I cover my ears with my hands and try to think fast. What rhymes with *basketball*? Zilch! And then I remember something Scott said, so I chant, "Ready, get set, nothing but net!" and toss the spell at myself. I've done enough spell-tossing to know they only last till midnight, but that's more than enough time to get me through gym class.

Mrs. Brinker says, "TEN!" just as I sprint back into the gym.

"I'm back! I needed my lucky socks!"

Mrs. Brinker glares at me, but I just grab the ball from Makayla and throw it toward the basket, which seems about a mile away. Darn it! The ball flies so low there's no way it's going in. Then, at the last second, it pops up and swishes through the net.

My mouth drops open, and so does Mrs. Brinker's.

"Do that again," she says.

Makayla can't believe her ears. "Mrs. Brinker! You said Lacey was getting detention."

"Quiet! Lacey's shooting."

Everyone in the gym looks at me as I pick up the ball. I start to sweat—I know I've got magic on my side, but this is still my worst bad-at-PE nightmare. I take a deep breath and shoot. The ball goes in the basket like it's being pulled by a magnet.

"Do it again," Mrs. Brinker orders.

Twenty-nine free throws later, the ball is *still* going in. Mrs. Brinker's eyes are about to pop out of her head—and the other kids are staring at me like I just grew a third ear. I drop the ball and ask Mrs. Brinker, "Do I still have to stay after school for remedial practice?"

Mrs. Brinker, still looking dazed, shakes her head. She tells me, "No, Lacey. That won't be necessary."

The bell rings, and I sprint to the locker room before she has a chance to change her mind.

CHAPTER

$\star$ $\star$ $\star$ $\star$ $\star$ $\star$
$\star$ $\star$ **11** $\star$ $\star$ $\star$
$\star$ $\star$ $\star$ $\star$ $\star$

After school, we all meet up in Sunny's backyard. Almost a whole day has gone by and I'm no closer to getting Gina married.

The girls look at me expectantly, and I have to tell them the truth. "I don't know how to find Gina her true love. Not a clue."

"Can't you just use magic?" Paige asks me. "When you were my fairy godmother, you turned that squirrel into a prince; he was handsome and really loved me."

"But only until midnight."

Sunny says, "My mom deserves better than a squirrel."

I nod. "And we need a *permanent* true love. Magic is always temporary."

Paige gets an idea. "What about your dad, Sunny? Maybe your mom still loves him. I saw this movie once where the kids get their parents back together."

"My dad's new wife wouldn't like that idea."

"Oh, I forgot about her," says Paige.

I kick the fence, which makes Fifi, the poodle next door, bark. I say, "This is so hard! We're never going to find anybody!"

Paige's phone buzzes, and she smiles as she reads a text. "It's from my father. He's still working at the hospital, but he wants me to meet him for dinner."

OMG!

I have a BRILLIANT idea. I know I have a lot of brilliant ideas, but this one is extra super special with sprinkles on top. "Sunny, your mom should marry Paige's dad!"

They're supposed to jump up and down and tell me how smart I am—but they don't. They just sit there staring.

"Think about it," I say. "They're not married to anybody and they've both got wonderful daughters—you'll be *sisters*!"

Paige says, "My dad's not ready to get married again!" But then she hesitates. "Well . . . I don't *think* he is."

And Sunny says, "It *would* be fun to have a sister."

"It can't hurt for Gina and Dr. Harrington to meet, can it?" I say.

Both girls shake their heads no, which isn't exactly jumping up and down, but it's going to have to do for now.

Trying to sound positive, I say, "We can do this! Maybe it'll be love at first sight."

"But my mom hasn't left the house all month," Sunny says. She turns to Paige. "How does your father feel about bathrobes?"

Paige smiles, but then she thinks of another problem. "My dad's working nights at the ER this week."

And, in a flash, I think of the answer. "It's simple. We send Gina to the ER with a big emergency."

Sunny asks, "What's the emergency?"

I say, "*You* are."

Half an hour later, Sunny, Paige and I rush into Gina's bedroom, where she's in bed watching more *Bridemonsters*.

I say, "Gina! Gina! Sunny needs to go to the hospital!"

Gina sits up, worried. "What's wrong?"

Paige says, "She's got a hundred-and-five-degree fever!" I show Gina the digital thermometer, which flashes 105°.

Sunny wobbles around the room, red and sweaty. Gina jumps out of bed and feels her forehead. "You're burning up!"

Sunny rasps, "Mommy! Why are there fish in the room?"

Gina says, "*Fish?*"

The fish were Sunny's idea; I thought they were silly, but boy, did they work.

Fifteen minutes after that, we're all rushing up to the emergency-room door. My plan has worked great—and it was so simple. All it took was a tiny bit of magic to make the thermometer read 105, plus Sunny running around the block until she was hot and sweaty. And now we're here, ready for Dr. Harrington to fall in love at first sight . . .

. . . with a woman in a bathrobe, no makeup, and unwashed crazy-lady hair. Love may be blind, but it can still smell.

I pull my wand out of my pocket and ad lib a spell: "Gina is a big mess! New hair, makeup, and dress!" I toss it just as she steps through the sliding door to the ER.

And when Gina comes out the other side, she looks like a movie star. Her hair is styled, her makeup is flawless, and she's wearing a cute little black dress. Oops—she's still got on her bunny slippers. But a fairy godmother can't think of everything.

Gina, so upset about Sunny that she doesn't even notice she's wearing different clothes, runs up to a nurse. "You've got to help us!"

"What's wrong?"

Sunny points at imaginary fish. "Look! Guppies! The whole room is full of guppies!"

That's all it takes. The nurse hurries us into an exam room.

A minute or two later, Dr. Harrington strides in, looking tall and handsome in a lab coat. And, like a character out of a romantic movie, he doesn't notice anyone else in the room, not me, not Sunny, not even his own daughter. He just stops and stares at Gina, and she stares back like she's hypnotized. (I'm so glad I changed her dress!)

This is working way better than I hoped. Love at first sight for sure!

I half expect him to sweep her into his arms and kiss her. So I'm shocked when instead, she crosses her arms and glares at him, and he crosses his arms, too. He says, in a curt voice, "Hello, Gina."

Gina says, every bit as curtly, "Hello, Stephen. I hope you're a better doctor than you were a driver."

"You're complaining already. Why doesn't that surprise me? There's a pediatrician on call tonight—let me get her." And he buzzes for the other doctor and leaves.

Whoa. What just happened? Not only do they know each other, they hate each other!

It takes us two hours to get out of the emergency room. The hospital people wanted to do a hundred different tests on Sunny until we finally admitted we were faking the whole thing. I'd describe the lecture we got from the doctor, but it would take about three pages.

Gina is *mad*! As she marches us back to the car, I almost expect to see smoke coming out of her ears.

Paige stayed behind at the hospital to have dinner with her dad—*lucky!*—so now it's just me, Sunny, and an angry Gina. I'm glad Katarina's at home with the pinch gnats. If she were in my pocket right now, she'd be kicking me.

Gina doesn't say a word until we get into the car. She doesn't start the engine and instead starts yelling. "What were you girls thinking? How could you fake something like that? You scared me to death!"

Sunny's probably going to get grounded.

"Did you think you were being funny? Well, you weren't! It was totally irresponsible! And Lacey, I'm calling your parents the second I get home."

Oops. I'm going to get grounded, too.

Then, miraculously, Sunny saves us. She takes Gina's hand and says, "Mom! I'm really, really sorry! But I had to do something to get you out of your bedroom. I've been so worried!"

Gina looks at Sunny, shocked. "You were worried about me?"

"Yes! You never get out of bed anymore and all you eat is wedding cake. You've stopped drawing—and you missed my karate class!" Sunny starts to cry.

All of Gina's anger about the emergency room evaporates. She hugs Sunny as tight as she can. "Oh, sweetie, I'm so sorry. I'll never miss one again. I know it's been hard for you lately. But I'll be better, I promise."

Wow. I may not have found Gina a husband, but at least she's going to try to act normal again. That's got to be a good thing.

The drive home is a lot calmer than I thought it was going to be. I even get brave enough to ask the big question: "You know Dr. Harrington?"

Gina rolls her eyes. "I dated him in high school. He asked me out to the prom—and then he got us lost on the way there. I knew the right exit, but he wouldn't listen to me, so we never made it to the dance." She sighs. "I saved for that prom dress for six months, and nobody ever saw it except for my parents and Stephen Harrington the Jerk." She pauses. "You guys think I'm being petty?"

Sunny and I both shake our heads. The prom is super important. I guess we can cross Dr. Harrington off the true-love list.

I have one more question for Gina: "Are you still going to call my parents and tell on me?"

"Not this time. But if you girls ever try anything like that again, you're grounded for life. Got it?"

Sunny and I both nod. *Whew!*

CHAPTER 12

The second I open the door of my house, Madison runs up to me in tears. "Somebody stole it!"

"Stole what?"

"Barbie's Ski Cabin! I came home and it was *gone!* They even took the hot tub!"

That's strange.

Mom's paying bills at the dining room table. "Madison, you know you're not supposed to leave your toys in the backyard. Now, go brush your teeth and I'll be right in."

"But, Mom! My ski cabin!"

"We'll look for it tomorrow. Brush your teeth."

Madison sniffles loudly and trudges away.

Mom asks me, "Did you have a good time with Sunny? What did you girls do?"

"Uh . . ." I pause, not wanting to lie. Mom knows I was spending the evening with Sunny and Gina—I texted her—but I left out the part about the emergency room. Finally I say, "Yes, we had a good time. We even got Gina out of the house!" Every word of that is true.

"That's great, sweetie. I told you she'd get better." Mom turns back to the bills, and I walk down the hall toward my bedroom.

When I find Julius crouched in front of my closed door, I sit down on the floor and scoop him up into my lap. Poor kitty. Every time I get mixed up with Katarina, he gets kicked out of my room. I hug him and say, "I still love you, Julius. You can go back in my room when this is all over."

He seems to understand, because he purrs and kneads my sweater. It's nice for me to have a little break, too. Fairy-godmothering is exhausting!

Suddenly, Julius's ears twitch. He hops off my lap and tries to peer under my bedroom door.

I put my ear to the door and hear faint, excited, *wheee!* sounds, kind of like preschoolers at the park. What the heck?

Julius claws at the door, desperate to get in and eat whatever's *whee*-ing. (He's definitely an attack cat.)

I gently push him away and slip into my room, closing the door behind me.

Inside, there's a sliver of light coming from under my closet door. As I walk up to it, the *wheeeeees* get louder.

I open the door—and see that the pinch gnats are having a party.

Splash! A couple of pinch gnats take turns diving into a Barbie-size hot tub full of strawberry Fanta, while others doze all around Barbie's Ski Cabin. Katarina ignores them as she sits on a Barbie lounge chair filing her nails.

I can't help laughing. *"You're* working hard."

"It's not as easy as it looks!"

"Geez, there are a lot of gnats! Are there more now than this morning?"

Katarina doesn't bother answering. She looks really cranky, like a mom who's been baby-sitting a whole flock of bratty kids. Which, when you think about it, is pretty much what she's been doing.

I tell her, "I'll sit with the gnats for a while if you want to watch TV or something."

"I'm fine! Remember, I'm babysitting them for you—to give you time to work! Is Gina married yet?"

"No!"

"The clock is ticking! Tick! Tick! Tick!"

"I have until Friday! And I got a lot done today."

Katarina picks up her notebook and pen. "What, exactly?"

"Well, I got Gina out of her house. And I found out that Dr. Harrington isn't her true love."

"That's all? There are seven billion people on this planet. You can't eliminate them one by one!"

"I'm looking as hard as I can! I thought you were going to give me hints."

"I've spent my whole day in a closet, and you expect me to give you hints? Wait, here's a hint: look harder! Now, close the door and stop bothering me!" She puts down the notebook and goes back to filing her nails. Wow, she's *ultra* cranky.

Another pinch gnat dives into the hot tub, and both Katarina and I get splashed.

"Watch it, you vermin!" Katarina yells. But she can't resist licking the sweet strawberry soda off her hand.

I wash the Fanta off my face in the bathroom I share with Madison. The door to Madison's room is open, and as Mom tucks her in to bed, Madison says, "But, Mommy! I know I didn't leave the ski cabin in the backyard!"

"We'll worry about it in the morning. Go to sleep now."

After Mom leaves, I hear Madison sniffling into her pillow.

Feeling guilty, I walk into Madison's room, sit down on her bed, and wipe away her tears. I think about telling her I've got the cabin, but it's too dangerous. She'd just blab to everyone, and there would be a lot more questions I wouldn't want to answer. Instead, I say, "I'm sure you'll find your ski cabin soon."

"Tomorrow?"

I don't want to promise that—the pinch gnats will still be using it. "Not tomorrow. Probably in four or five days. Saturday morning at the latest."

"But I want it now! I promised Barbie she could go skiing!" Madison tears up again.

"Don't cry," I say. "Maybe tonight you'll dream about Barbie and the cabin."

"No, I won't. I only ever dream about ballet class and puppies." Tears slide down her cheeks.

I tell her, "Close your eyes and think ski thoughts."

After making sure her eyes are closed, I pull the wand out of my pocket and softly chant, "Dreams we'll be havin' in our own ski cabin." Then I toss the spell.

"Okay, Madison! Open your eyes!" When Madison opens them, her room has been transformed into a real cabin. The walls are wood, snow falls outside the window, and a fire burns in the stone fireplace that sits where her dresser used to be. I can't help it—I'm impressed with myself. I ask her, "What do you think?"

"This isn't Barbie's cabin. Barbie's cabin is *pink*."

True. Also plastic. Five-year-olds are hard to impress.

But Madison looks around the room and then snuggles down under her covers. "This is nice, too. I like this dream. And I'm glad you're dreaming with me."

I sit with Madison in the mountain cabin until she falls asleep. While I wait, I think about what the fairies have asked me to do. What if I don't pass the wedding test? Will my family hate me, too, just like everyone else in the world will?

And if I do pass the wedding test, in four days I'll get sent away for a hundred years. How will that work? Will the fairies make it so Madison won't even remember me? And Mom and Dad, and Sunny, and Paige? Oh, and Julius, too. It will be like I was never born!

Maybe I can visit them in their dreams. Madison will dream about a ski cabin with snow outside and a cozy fire, and a sister she loved once but has now forgotten. And the sister in the dream will sit holding her hand, just like I am now.

I wipe away more tears from Madison's sleeping face. Only they're not her tears, they're mine.

CHAPTER 13

Tuesday morning, I leave Katarina in the closet babysitting the pinch gnats again, and Sunny, Paige, and I walk to school together.

I tell the girls, "I don't know what to do! It's never this complicated in the fairy tales. All the fairy godmother has to do is make dresses and find coaches. The prince just shows up—why can't it be like that?"

Paige says, "Well, maybe there's a prince right under our noses."

Sunny crosses her eyes and looks down toward the tip of her nose. Trying not to giggle, she says, "I don't see a prince."

The problem is, neither do I.

All day in school, I think about finding Gina a prince. And all day, I give wrong answers in class.

In math, "Maybe a fireman" is not the correct answer to the story problem about two trains leaving Chicago.

In World Cultures, "Maybe that cute guy at the yogurt store" is not the correct answer to "Who is the prime minister of Australia?"

In French, "Monsieur Smith, are you married?" is *not* the correct translation of *"Òu est la bibliothèque?"*

Finally, I make it to PE, which is my last class today. At least there won't be any questions here for me to answer wrong. But there could be something worse—if I play as badly as I usually do, I may get remedial practice from Mrs. Brinker after school.

So, just before I walk out on the gym floor, I chant, "Ready, get set, nothing but net," and toss the spell at myself, and I'm good to go.

I'm more than good! I'm great! I make every shot, even the ones where I'm barely looking.

So I'm surprised—and unhappy—when Mrs. Brinker pulls me aside. "Lacey, I want you to stay after class today."

Oh, drat! How good do I have to be *not* to get remedial practice?

All the other kids file out, and Makayla gives me an extra-big smirk as I make one last, desperate attempt to get out of staying after school. "But Mrs. Brinker, I'm getting better!"

"Just stay here," Mrs. Brinker says. She leaves the gym without another word.

So I stand against the wall as the seconds tick away on the gym clock and the boys start filing in for basketball practice.

Scott, dressed in a uniform so new that it still has the store creases in it, walks up to me smiling. "Lacey! Did you come to watch me practice?"

"I'm waiting for Mrs. Brinker. Is today your first practice with the team?"

"Yes. And there's a game on Friday night, so I've got to be good!"

"You're going to be a starter, I know it."

"I hope so. You coming to the game?"

I'm about to say yes when I remember that I'm going to be at a wedding. Luckily, I don't have to say anything, because the tallest boy on the team, Dylan Hernandez, throws Scott a ball and they start shooting hoops.

I keep waiting for Mrs. Brinker. Just when I think she's forgotten about me, she shows up with Principal Nazarino and the tall, friendly-looking boys' basketball coach, Mr. Overdale. Principal Nazarino bends down to take off her high heels, which aren't allowed in the gym, and the coach holds out a hand to steady her.

They all walk over and stare down at me for a moment like I'm a bug they've never seen before. Then Mrs. Brinker picks up a basketball and shoves it in my hands. "Lacey! Shoot!"

Feeling like a bug, I just stare at her.

"Don't waste our time! Shoot!"

So I throw the ball, and it swishes through the net with barely a sound.

"Way to go, Lacey!" Scott shouts. I can't help blushing.

Coach Overdale claps his hands on my shoulders. "I have just one question for you. How would you like to try out for the basketball team?"

"What?"

Principal Nazarino says, "Try out for the team."

"But the girls already finished their season!" I say.

Coach Overdale smiles. "Yes, they have. But Mrs. Brinker has told me how good you are. I want you to try out for the boys' team."

"You'd be the first girl on a boys' team in the entire state!" Principal Nazarino says.

The three adults all smile and nod at me. And I have to admit it, being on the team would be pretty cool. Dad would be so proud of me.

The coach blows his whistle and waves the boys over. "Lacey is going to practice with you! Let's see what she can do."

I hear cheers and whoops, and see Scott giving me a big thumbs-up. I start grinning—and then it hits me. I *can't* try out for the team. I have a wedding to plan! Besides, it would be cheating to get on the team by magic. So I say, "I don't think—"

"Don't think, play!" Coach Overdale says. He shoves me toward the boys and tosses me the ball.

Well, this shouldn't be too hard. If I'm not any good, I won't make the team.

So, for the next ten minutes, I try to be bad, but I can't. With the magic spell on me, and no matter how much I try to fight it, I'm the best player ever. I dribble like an NBA all-star. I make every shot I take. I'm so good the boys barely get to touch the ball at all.

By the time coach blows his whistle to give us a break, all the boys are panting and out of breath, and I haven't even broken a sweat.

Coach Overdale shakes my hand. "Lacey, welcome to the team! I want you to suit up for practice every day this week—and

you're going to play in Friday's game!" Mrs. Brinker and Principal Nazarino high-five each other.

Oh, puke! This is just what I don't need!

I have to spend the rest of the afternoon playing basketball with my new team. And all this basketball practice is not going to help Gina one bit.

CHAPTER 14

It's Meatloaf Madness Night at the Hungry Moose, and the dining room is packed when I get there. On MMN, it's my job to refill the ketchup bottles, so I head straight for the storeroom.

But before I get halfway across the room, Dad comes out of the kitchen wheeling a serving cart with a huge, round meatloaf on it. He's used bacon to make stripes and to write out the word *Spalding.* OMG. It's a meatloaf basketball!

Dad sticks a sparkler into the meatloaf, lights it, and raps on the cart to get everyone's attention. "Ladies, gentlemen, and sports fans! This afternoon I got a call from Coach Overdale, who tells me that my wonderful, talented, amazing daughter Lacey has just made the boys' basketball team. So, tonight—free meatloaf for everybody!" There's wild applause. I think it's mostly for the free food.

Dad gives me a huge hug. "I'm so proud of you, honey, and on Friday, I'm going to be in the front row, cheering louder than anybody! Coach Overdale says you're the best natural player he's ever seen."

Make that best *un*natural player. But Dad looks sooo happy—I've got to let him down easy. "I'm not very good. I might not even get to play."

"That's not what the coach says!"

With a happy grin, he stabs a knife into the meatloaf basket-ball and starts to serve.

"Your father gave you a *meatloaf?*" Katarina sits on my dresser smearing cold cream on her face.

"Yes, with a sparkler on top."

"This modern age is ridiculous. In my day, fathers gave their daughters diamonds, tapestries, and real estate. Now you get ground beef. It's a sad, sad decline, if you ask me."

"My dad makes the best meatloaf in town."

"I stand corrected. Chopped meat is much better than mere jewelry."

I'm not sure if Katarina's insulting me or Dad—but it's probably both.

Katarina says, "How was your day?"

"Terrible. I still haven't found Gina's true love."

"You're just not very good at this, are you?"

"No, I'm not." Feeling tired and hopeless, I pull off my sweater and go to the closet to hang it up.

Katarina stops me. "Don't go in there!"

"Why not?"

"I just got the pinch gnats to sleep! They've been fussy all day. Oh, and we need more soda."

"I checked—we're out of Fanta. I think we've got some ginger ale."

"Fine. They're bugs—they'll drink what I give them." Katarina finishes with the cold cream and sits on the edge of the dresser. "While the little monsters are sleeping, let me give you some more unofficial advice."

I wish she could have given me this unofficial advice yesterday, but I guess she was too cranky.

Katarina says, "Pay attention! Your wand isn't just for spells, it can also function as a love locator. Tomorrow, when you see a man who might be a match, point your wand and say, 'Shall this man be Gina's true love?' If he's the one, your wand will tell you."

"It doesn't have to rhyme?"

"No, it's a question, not a spell."

Wow, a test for true love. "Thank you, Katarina! If I can find Gina a man, all my problems are solved."

"No, they're not."

"What do you mean?"

"I *mean*, have you found a church? A minister? Flowers? A dress? Please tell me you at least have the dress. You can have the shabbiest wedding ever, but if the dress is pretty, nothing else matters."

Wow. I've got a lot to do.

I text Sunny and Paige: *MEET ME AT THE FOUNTAIN BEFORE SCHOOL.*

Then I start Googling like a maniac.

First thing the next morning, I make sure Katarina has a day's supply of ginger ale for the pinch gnats. Then I kiss Mom and Dad good-bye and head out the door.

Just like I expected it to be, the park is as quiet and empty as always when I meet Sunny and Paige there. I turn on my phone and tell them, "We need to choose a wedding dress. There were hundreds of pretty ones online, but I found three I loved."

Sunny looks confused as I flip through four pictures. "You said there were three."

"Madison picked one, too."

Paige points at a picture of a princessy dress with pink lace, a poufy net skirt, and huge embroidered roses all over it. "Madison picked *this* one. Kind of over the top, isn't it?"

"Madison *loves* over the top! She saw me looking at dresses and wouldn't go to bed till I bookmarked her favorite." I hold up the phone to show the dresses I like side by side. "That leaves three. Let's vote."

Sunny points to a dress that has a huge hoop skirt and off-the-shoulder sleeves. "That one!"

Paige's favorite is a white dress that a Greek goddess might have worn: simple, elegant, and flowing. In the picture, the bride is even leaning against a Greek column.

And I choose the third dress, which has beautiful lace at the neck, a long, long train, and a gardenia headpiece instead of a veil. "We've all picked something different," I say. "How are we going to decide?

Sunny says, "It's my mom, so I get to choose."

Paige says, "I don't want to sound like a snob, but I should choose, because I have the best taste."

And I say, "*I* should choose, because I'm the fairy godmother, and the fairy godmother knows best."

"So why did you even bother asking us?" Sunny says.

Paige studies the three dresses. "You can't tell from a picture, anyway. You have to try things on. Everyone knows that."

I didn't.

Sunny holds the phone in front of her and does a fake model walk. "Does this help you decide?"

Not really, but I get an idea. "Let's see . . . What rhymes with *dress*?"

The girls look at me, confused, as I chant, "Let's model each dress so we'll have success!" and toss the spell at the three of us.

Poof! There are three flashes of light, and then we're each wearing the wedding dress we like best. Paige's dress even came complete with the Greek column from the picture. I'm that good.

"Oooh!" Sunny says as she twirls in the hoop skirt. She puts on a fake Southern accent and drawls, "Ah declare, ah am the most beautiful bride of all!"

Paige lets the white silk of her gown slide between her fingers. "This is gorgeous!"

And I look behind me and see a long white satin train that stretches halfway down the path. As I walk, the train gets caught in a bush. Maybe a fifteen-foot train was not the best choice.

Paige takes a step toward me to help with my train and then says, "Uh-oh."

"What is it?"

"The column is part of the ensemble." (And it's just like Paige to know a word like *ensemble*.)

"Please tell me you're kidding."

But sure enough, the tall Greek column is glued to the back of Paige's white silk dress. Paige takes another step and the column comes with her. "It's not heavy—it's like the Styrofoam we use in art class. Help me get it off."

Sunny reaches for the column, but her hoop skirt is wider than her arms can stretch. So I grab the column and try to pull it off. It doesn't budge—not one bit.

Sunny, positive as usual, says, "Except for the column, Paige's dress is prettiest! My mom would look *beautiful* in that one."

Okay, decision made. The day of the wedding I'll make the Greek goddess dress for Gina, minus the column.

And then I think of something: godmother spells last till midnight.

I used a spell to make these dresses.

Oops.

CHAPTER 16

Paige, Sunny and I walk up the steps of the school in our white wedding gowns. We're trying not to draw attention to ourselves, but it's impossible. After all, I'm dragging a fifteen-foot train, Sunny's bumping into kids with her hoop skirt, and Paige has a six-foot-high Styrofoam column stuck to her back.

"You really need to think before you do these spells!" Paige says, as cranky as Katarina.

"I know, I know. I'm sorry."

Sunny tugs at her skirt. "How did people ever wear these things? You couldn't even ride a bike!" Wham! She bumps into Marcie Dunphy, the smallest girl in our class, and knocks her down. "Oh, I'm so sorry!"

Marcie stares at us for a second, then picks herself up and scurries away.

When I feel a yank on my train, I'm sure it's one of the boys giving me a hard time. "STOP THAT!" I turn around and see it's *not* one of the boys; it's Principal Nazarino.

She looks at the three of us, baffled. "What are you girls doing! Go home and change, *now!*"

That's just what we *can't* do. So I say, "All my other clothes were dirty, so my mom made me wear this."

Principal Nazarino scowls at me. "And what about Sunny and Paige? Were all their clothes dirty, too? And is that a *column*?"

I've made a lot of excuses in my life, but "My clothes were dirty" has got to be the lamest one. (Even worse than the time I tried to get out of gym by saying my arm was broken and I was wearing a special invisible cast.) Principal Nazarino's going to give us all detention, for sure.

Sunny elbows me. "Just tell her the truth, Lacey!"

"*What?*" I whisper to Sunny, "Are you crazy? I can't tell her I'm a fairy godmo—"

Very loudly, Sunny says, "No, the truth! About how we're entering the mascot competition today."

Principal Nazarino, Paige, and I stare at Sunny like she's crazy. But Sunny just punches the air with her fist and shouts, "GO, BRIDES!"

Wow, Sunny thinks fast. But that's the stupidest idea for a mascot I've ever heard.

"This is a joke, right?" Principal Nazarino says.

Sunny shakes her head. The only thing I can do is play along. I punch the air, too, and shout, "LINCOLN BRIDES RULE!"

And Paige uses every bit of her cheerleader skills and shouts, "Give me a *B*!"

Sunny and I shout, *"B!"*

"Give me an *R*!"

"R!"

"Give me an *I*!"

"I!"

Principal Nazarino waves her hands. "Stop! I get it! But the mascot competition isn't till this afternoon, so take those costumes off."

Without batting an eyelash, Paige says, "These dresses are custom made, and we had to be sewn into them this morning. Look, I even glued the column on. It took hours."

I *love* my godmother posse! My girls are the best! But is Nazarino buying it?

The principal walks around us, studying the gowns. To my relief, she smiles. "These dresses are really beautiful—I've seen ones just like them online."

That makes sense, since that's where I copied them from. I wonder what Principal Nazarino's doing looking at wedding gowns? That seems way too girlie-girl for her.

Principal Nazarino says, "All right, I'll let you keep them on. But if the dresses disrupt your classes, I'm sending you home until this afternoon. Good luck with the competition."

Principal Nazarino walks away, and Sunny does a little tap dance. At least I think that's what she's doing—I can't really tell, because I can't see her feet under all that dress. She says, "Am I a genius or what?"

I say, "You're a genius."

Paige frowns, thinking of something. "A genius who just entered us in a mascot competition in front of the whole school. The kids are going to laugh at us."

Sunny stops tap-dancing and frowns, too. She asks me, "Can you do a spell to make Principal Nazarino forget that we're supposed to be in the show?"

"I could try . . . but I'd be messing with her brain. What if I exploded it or something?"

Paige asks, "How hard could a memory spell be?"

"You're the one with a column stuck to your back. You tell me!"

"You'd *totally* explode her brain."

I nod. "It's not that big a problem. We'll just hide in the janitor's bathroom."

Suddenly, there's a surprised voice behind us. *"Sunny? Girls?"*

We all turn and see Gina, who holds an armload of art supplies.

"Mom! What are you doing here?" Sunny says.

"I'm volunteering for the art class. I've missed a lot lately, and

I want to get back in the swing of things." She stares in disbelief at our wedding dresses. "What the heck are you girls wearing?"

I say, "Uh . . . we're going to be in the competition to choose the new school mascot this afternoon."

I'm worried that the wedding dresses are going to make Gina sad, but she looks them over and laughs. "What a funny idea. If I've learned anything from *Bridemonsters*, it's that there's nothing more vicious than a bride. What time is the competition?"

"Two o'clock," Sunny says.

"I'll be back this afternoon with my camera! I can't wait!" Gina disappears into the art class.

Sunny, Paige and I stare at each other. "I guess we're going to be Bridemonsters," I say.

Sunny and Paige nod.

Mr. Griffith, the music teacher, is in charge of today's competition, so we go to the music room to sign up.

Mr. Griffith *loves* our wedding dresses. "These costumes are Tony-worthy." He taps on Paige's column. "Like Brecht with Dada-esque undertones." (That's the way Mr. Griffith talks. You're lucky if you understand one in three things he says.) Then he frowns. "You girls were supposed to sign up by last Friday."

That's good! Maybe we can still get out of doing this. I say, "We missed the signup day? Too bad! Darn it so much. But rules are rules." And then I put on a fake sad expression.

"Wait! I'm not a dictator, and rules are meant to be broken." (Since when? Mr. Griffith kicks people out of his class for having mismatched socks!) He looks at our dresses again and chuckles. "The Lincoln Bridemonsters. How clever! Show up at two and give the school your best!"

The fake sad expression was probably a mistake.

CHAPTER 17

Mr. Griffith may love our dresses, but no one else in school does. The teachers all yell at Sunny because her hoop skirt blocks the aisles, and Paige can't even sit down—all she can do is lean against her column.

And imagine walking around in a wedding dress with a fifteen-foot train! All morning, people are either tripping on it or trying to ride it.

I *do* remember to use the wand as a love locator a couple of times. I aim it at the assistant principal and ask, "Shall this man be Gina's true love?" The wand makes an annoying little *raspberry* sound. The question sounds fancy, but the answer is rude.

Then I aim the wand at the janitor, at the nerdy guy who fixes the school computers, and at the man who refills the vending machines. The wand raspberrys all of them, and the sound gets a little ruder each time. I finally put the wand back in my pocket. What good is a love locator if the answer is always no?

Between second and third period, Scott comes up to me in the hallway and says, "Congratulations, Lacey!" But he doesn't look happy.

He doesn't think I'm actually getting married, does he? That's not even legal.

"You *are* better than me," Scott says.

I'm confused. Maybe the dress is cutting off the flow of blood to my brain. "Better? At what?"

"Basketball. The coach just told me: you made the A-team. You're starting in Friday's game."

"You are, too, right?"

"No. I got cut. But I'm going to come watch you win."

He got cut from the team? That's so wrong—Scott deserves to play in the game. I'm only good because I'm cheating with magic.

Scott pats my back. "Way to go." And he doesn't mean it sarcastically, he really means it—he's happy for me even if he's sad for himself. He's so nice, and I'm so awful.

What if I told Scott the truth? What if I told him I'm a fairy godmother? Would that make him feel better about being cut from the team . . .

. . . because I cheated?

No, it wouldn't. This is really messed up.

At the end of Mr. Carver's science class, it's my turn to feed the mice. So instead of leaving for lunch, I stay behind and get out the Mouse Chow.

I have trouble getting the container open, because my fingernails are so chewed up from my worrying about Scott—not to mention Gina. How am I ever going to find her a husband by Friday?

The window near me is open, and the frogs in the woods next to the school are croaking like crazy, the way they always do.

I stare out the window, thinking. In the fairy tale, there's a frog that turns into a prince when a girl kisses him. I know this is probably just a story—but I never believed in fairy godmothers before, either. If the story were true, I'd have a prince for Gina with one kiss. A prince who won't change back at midnight, because he's really human underneath.

It's a crazy idea, but it's the only one I have.

I pull out my wand and point it toward the woods. "Gina needs a princely frog. If you're there, get off your log."

A moment after I toss the spell, *WHOOSH!* Something zooms through the window, right at my head. I duck. Is it a frog prince?

No, it's Katarina. She plops down on a desk, breathing hard.

I ask, "What's wrong? Why aren't you home babysitting the pinch gnats?"

"Because they're *gone*!"

"What?"

"I opened the closet door this morning, and they swarmed out and knocked me down. Lacey, you were right. There *are* more of them! They've been laying eggs!"

"In my closet? Yuck!"

"I *wish* they were still in your closet, because they all flew out the window. I assumed they were on their way to find you. They're not here?"

"No."

Katarina frowns. "Odd. They should be swarming all over you by now."

"Maybe they found a hummingbird feeder."

"Are there a lot of those?" Katarina asks.

"Everyone in town has one."

"Well, that will probably keep them occupied for a while, but they could show up anytime."

"Should we try to find them?"

"Don't worry. When the last drop of hummingbird food is gone, they'll find you." Katarina's been so distracted that she only just now notices my dress. She says, "What in the name of glitter are you wearing?"

"I was testing wedding dresses."

"And you forgot about the midnight rule."

Now might be a good time to change the subject. "Katarina? Are there really frog princes?"

"Of course not. That was just the frogs trying to impress people. Why?"

I'm not going to tell her I was stupid enough to believe in enchanted frogs. "Just wondering."

Between the wedding dresses, the mascot competition, and the missing pinch gnats, this is turning out to be a very strange day.

CHAPTER 18

As kids and teachers take their seats in the bleachers for the mascot competition, Sunny, Paige, and I wait in chairs on the gym floor along with the other candidates. Katarina hides behind the gardenias in my hair.

There's over a dozen of us, including a Spartan with painted-on abs, a Viking with horns and a shield, and a scary-looking grizzly bear. The grizzly-bear costume is the most professional. The father of the kid who's wearing it owns a car lot that has "Bear-y Good Deals," and people get their picture taken with the bear when they buy a car.

I hear a weird clanking sound—maybe somebody's competing as a knight or a robot. But it's Gina, with three cameras around her neck. She rushes up and starts taking pictures, blinding us with camera flashes. "Girls, let's see those dresses!"

Suddenly remembering why we were looking at dresses in

the first place, I ask her, "Which dress do you like best?"

Gina looks at the three of us. "I could never decide! You all look lovely!"

Drat. She doesn't want to hurt anybody's feelings by choosing one dress over the others, but I need her to decide. "If *you* had to wear one, which one would you choose? We have a bet about it."

Gina looks at the dresses again and finally points at Paige's. "That one, I think. Only, without the column."

Yay! The day of the wedding, I know which gown to magic up for her. As Katarina always says, the dress is crucial.

Mr. Griffith walks up to a microphone and taps it. "Quiet, everybody, Quiet!"

Gina hugs all three of us and takes a seat in the bleachers next to Principal Nazarino and Coach Overdale.

I can't believe I'm going to be a Bridemonster in front of the whole school. This is like a bad dream.

Mr. Griffith continues, "Today we're here to choose a new mascot for Lincoln Middle School. It is a decision that will reverberate down through generations of students! So, do not take this lightly. After the presentations, there will be a secret ballot. May the best mascot win!"

Because Paige, Sunny, and I signed up last, we get to sit and watch the other kids go up to the microphone to give their version of a mascot cheer. All *we're* going to do is Paige's "Give me a *B!*" cheer. But still, this is scary.

The Spartan kid steps up to the microphone and raises a cardboard sword: "We're the Lincoln Spartans! We cut off heads! We hack off arms! Blood will spatter at every game! We rip out their insides, and then we—"

Mr. Griffith grabs the microphone. "Thank you. That was very vivid. Next!"

The audience really seems to like the Viking, even though his long blond beard falls off when he gives his cheer. And when the grizzly stands up and roars, everyone roars right back. I'm relieved to see that the audience isn't too picky; everybody's happy to be out of class.

The next-to-last kid is a skinny sixth-grader named Martin Shembly, who wears a blue polyester uniform and carries a violin. Martin goes to the microphone and says, "I think we should be the Lincoln Trekkers. The *Star Trek* theme is very inspiring. Let me play it for you now."

It's the nerdiest thing I've ever seen, and that includes Dad's monthly chess-club meetings at the Hungry Moose.

Sunny leans over to me and whispers, "He's really good!" But she's the only one who thinks so. *Star Trek* plus violin is too much for the crowd: they start booing. Principal Nazarino stands up and glares, and everybody shuts up. But the mood of the crowd has definitely turned ugly.

And Sunny, Paige, and I are up next. *Gulp.*

As we walk up to the microphone in our wedding dresses,

there are giggles from the crowd. I'm so sorry that I've gotten Paige and Sunny into this (not to mention myself).

But Paige is both a popular girl and a cheerleader, and she takes over. She grabs the microphone and says, "Any school can have a boring mascot. We want to do something different! Something that will get us noticed! We're the Bridemonsters—and Bridemonsters never, ever stop till they get what they want! And we want to WIN! Do you hear me? *We want to win!*"

The kids look at her, not sure what they think about this. Then Scott stands up and starts to applaud. A moment later, Dylan Hernandez and the rest of the basketball team stand up. And two moments later, the whole crowd is cheering for the Bridemonsters.

This is kind of awesome.

Paige motions for quiet, and because she's Paige, she gets it. (Talk about a good friend to have!) She looks at me and Sunny and shouts, "Give me a *B*!"

Sunny and I shout back, *"B!"*

"Give me an *R*!"

Just as Sunny and I are about to shout back, there's a loud *RIBBET* in the gym—

—and a large green frog hops across the floor. There are laughs from all the kids, but the frog doesn't pay any attention. He hops to the edge of the bleachers and stares with his beady little eyes like he's looking for someone.

And then the frog hops right into Gina's lap.

Other moms would have shrieked or jumped, but Gina just laughs. "Hello, there, Mr. Frog," she says, picking him up to look at him.

The frog leans forward and kisses her on the lips.

"We don't know each other well enough for you to do that," Gina says. This gets a huge laugh from the crowd.

I stare at the frog. Is he here because of my spell? Maybe Katarina's wrong about there being no frog princes. OMG!

But nothing happens. The frog stays a frog, and the kids all start making loud kissing sounds.

Mr. Griffith claps his hands for attention. "People, please!"

Gina stands up and gives Mr. Griffith a little wave of apology. "I'll put him outside."

She carries the frog to the side door that leads to the parking lot. When she opens it, there are more frogs waiting on the sidewalk.

The frogs croak and ribbet with excitement—and then leap right toward Gina's face. I may not have found Gina a prince, but I've sure found her a lot of frogs.

Gina's still not freaking out. (I know *I* would be.) She starts tossing the frogs back outside, and Coach Overdale jumps up and runs over to help.

As everyone in the auditorium stares at the frog-tossing,

Katarina yanks on my ear and whispers, "Is there any spell you want to tell me about?"

"All right! I tried to find a frog prince. But you said there weren't any, so I thought I was okay!"

"You idiot! All frogs *think* they're princes. Don't you know that? Go get that door shut before every amorous amphibian in the forest shows up!"

Katarina calls me an idiot a lot, but this time it stings, because it's sort of true. With my face burning, I wrap the train of my wedding dress around myself and walk over to the door to help Gina and the coach herd the frogs outside.

Sunny and Paige start to follow me, but Principal Nazarino stops them. "Sunny, Paige! You girls hand out the ballots for the competition. And everybody else, QUIET!"

There aren't all that many frogs, just a couple dozen. Gina, the coach, and I finally grab the last of them and carry them out into the parking lot. I push the auditorium door shut with my butt so no more frogs can get inside.

Even though the frogs keep jumping at Gina's face, she just laughs. "This is *nutty*!"

"No kidding!" Katarina whispers.

Okay, I admit it was a stupid spell. But it could have been worse.

Then I hear a weird sound from the edge of the parking lot.

Oh no. Oh no! OH NO!

It's the sound of hundreds of frogs croaking at once. And they're all hopping straight for Gina.

One frog is cute.

A dozen frogs is annoying.

A hundred frogs is *scary.*

CHAPTER

19

A green river of frogs engulfs us.

Not *us*—the frog river flows past me and the coach, and swirls like a whirlpool around Gina. Because of my stupid spell, she's the one they want.

Gina has been calm so far, but now she screams as hundreds of frogs try to kiss her. She tries to run—but she can't take a step without squishing a frog. So she covers her head with her arms and huddles down as the frogs pile on top of her.

I pick up frogs and toss them away, but for every one I toss, another three jump on. "You're not princes, you're just frogs!" I shout. But they don't pay any attention to me.

Finally, the coach gets as close as he can to Gina. "Take my hand!" he yells. She reaches out—

—and he pulls her up and into his arms, so fast that the frogs drop to the ground.

As the coach carries Gina, he looks like a knight on the cover of one of those romance novels my grandma reads. And Gina looks like the damsel in distress.

With the frogs still jumping all around them, the coach runs across the parking lot, opens the door of his white Mustang, and gets them both inside. A moment later, the car is just a mound of green.

Katarina flutters near my face, *tsk*-ing.

"This is horrible!" I say. "Gina and the coach are going to be stuck in the car till midnight!"

"Probably."

I look at Katarina with a faint flicker of hope. "Only probably?"

Katarina asks, "What exactly was the spell you used?"

"'Gina needs a princely frog. If you're there, get off your log.'"

Katarina sits on my shoulder, thinking. "Since the frogs aren't really princes, just conceited, it's a breakable spell."

"So, how do I break it?"

"You have to make them forget the spell by giving them something they want more."

What do frogs want? They probably only want lily pads—and bugs. Lots and lots of bugs. I almost wish the pinch gnats were here; there's a zillion of them, especially since they've been laying eggs in my closet.

The pinch gnats! I know what I need to do!

I cup my hands around my mouth and shout question after question at Katarina. "Why is the sky blue? What did I have for dinner last Tuesday? Who invented Silly String? When is Sunny's birthday? What is the capital of Uruguay? Why does it always rain when you're having a picnic? What's the world's highest mountain? How much wood would a woodchuck chuck if a woodchuck could chuck wood? How many Barbies does Madison have? When was the first Super Bowl? Where is the world's longest river?"

By now Katarina has her hands clamped over her ears. "Have you gone insane? Sit down and put your head between your legs!"

I shout even louder, not even bothering to look at Katarina anymore. I want to be so loud that anyone—or *anything*—nearby can hear me. "Does putting your head between your legs cure insanity? Do you know the way to San Jose? How does a Magic 8 Ball work? If you swallow gum, does it really stay in your stomach? What is my aunt Ginny's actual age? Is there intelligent life in the universe?"

"There's no intelligent life *here*! Why are you asking all these ridiculous questions? If the pinch gnats were here, they'd pinch you to death!" And Katarina finally gets it. "Oh," she says. "You *want* the pinch gnats to come."

"Yes. BECAUSE AREN'T THE PINCH GNATS REALLY JUST TASTY BUGS?"

With this final question, a bright red cloud of angry, buzzing gnats rises over the top of the school. (They've probably drained every hummingbird feeder in town.) Those gnats must have laid a lot of eggs in my closet, because it's a *big* swarm. And the swarm is heading straight for the one who asked Katarina all those questions.

Me.

I dash behind the frog-covered car and wait. What if my plan doesn't work?

The pinch gnats zoom toward me from the other side of the car—and hundreds of frogs stop thinking, Gina! Gina! and start thinking, Lunch! Lunch!

As the swarm passes over them, the frogs' long, sticky tongues dart out to eat the pinch gnats like they are the most delicious bugs ever. In less than a second, the frogs gobble up almost all of them.

The gnats that *don't* get eaten fly into the woods, and all the hungry frogs hop off the car and go after them.

A minute later, there's not a single gnat or a single frog in the parking lot, just me and Katarina. Instead of a deafening roar of *ribbets* and buzzing, now there's just wonderful silence.

Katarina flies up to me and perches on a gardenia in my hair again. "Not the way I would have done it, but that worked."

"Are the pinch gnats coming back?" I ask.

"Not unless frog poop can fly."

EW! I shudder, but not for long. Because that's actually pretty great—I just solved two problems at once. No more frogs, and no more pinch gnats. I tell Katarina, "So now I can ask you all the questions I want—and you can give me all sorts of help!"

"Not so fast, missy. I'm happy bending the rules, but I'm not going to *break* the rules, pinch gnats or no pinch gnats. I'll give you suggestions. Such as, I suggest you tell Gina that the frogs have gone to lunch."

Good idea. I knock on the door of Coach Overdale's car. "You can come out!"

Gina cautiously opens the door.

"It's all right! They're gone," I say.

Gina and the coach get out of the car and look at the empty parking lot. Gina lets out a huge sigh of relief, and then gives Coach Overdale a big, grateful hug. "Thank you so much!"

He hugs her back, blushing a little but smiling.

Then I get a GREAT idea. The coach is nice. He has a good job. He really likes kids. And, even if he's got a sunburn and not much hair, he's handsome. Is he the man for Gina?

Right then, Principal Nazarino opens the auditorium door

and walks over. "Coach Overdale? Are you ever planning on rejoining us?"

I quickly pull the wand out of my sleeve and ask it in a whisper, "Shall this man be Gina's true love?"

Please, please, please, don't raspberry the coach!

The wand glows pink and makes a *ping-ping-ping* like a slot machine paying off. I say quietly to Katarina, "The answer is yes! Coach Overdale is Gina's prince!"

I've found the prince.

Now all I have to do is get them married. In three days.

CHAPTER 20

Half an hour later, Sunny, Paige, and I pile into Gina's old Hyundai. It's hard enough squishing Sunny's hoop skirt into the Hyundai's backseat, but for a while it looks like there is no way that Paige's column will fit. Finally, Gina opens the sunroof and Paige stands with her head—and her column—poking out. All the way to Sunny's house, Paige waves at people on the street like she's practicing for a parade.

When we girls go into Sunny's backyard to talk, Fifi barks at us through the fence. Katarina tells her, "Yes, a fifteen-foot train is excessive. *So* five years ago." Fifi barks in agreement.

Sheesh! Everyone's a stylist!

While Gina was around, I couldn't say anything about my exciting news about the love-locator test and Coach Overdale. But now I tell the girls every wonderful detail.

Paige and I both look at Sunny—after all, the coach is going to be her new stepfather. Sunny thinks about it for just a moment, and then smiles. "He's *way* better than Dwight!"

I breathe a big sigh of relief.

"So, what's next?" Paige asks.

"Well, they're getting married on Friday, so I guess they should go out on a date tonight," I say.

Katarina snorts. "It better be a *fantastic* date, if they're getting married on Friday."

I say, "Okay, Katarina. We need fantastic. What would be a fantastic date?"

Katarina doesn't hesitate. "Invading Italy!"

We all look at her, confused.

Katarina scratches her head. "It was that man in the hat . . . What was his name? He was very defensive about being short. They named a pastry after him?"

Sunny guesses, "Twinkie?"

"No . . . *Napoleon!* That's it! He was trying to figure out how to get Josephine's attention, and I suggested he send an army to Rome. She was wowed!"

"Gina is not Napoleon, Katarina," I say patiently. For a fairy, she can be a little dense sometimes. "We need to think of something simpler—and where people don't get killed."

Over the next half hour, Paige, Sunny, and I come up with a lot of ideas for a perfect date: horseback riding, a picnic, hiking, or a hot-air-balloon ride. None of them seems right.

Finally, Katarina raises her hand. "May I make one teensy-weensy suggestion?"

I brace myself for whatever rude thing she's about to say.

"Why don't you talk to Gina?"

That's actually a really good idea. (I'm sure I would've thought of it eventually.) I say, "Let's go talk to her right now!"

Katarina shakes her head. "No, Lacey, *you* go talk to her right now. You're Gina's fairy godmother. Not Paige, not Sunny, not me. Go find out what her dream date is."

When I get inside, I find Gina in her workroom, sketching with colored chalk. "Hi, Lacey," she says, looking up for just a second. "I haven't drawn anything in six weeks—but those frogs inspired me."

"You're going to do a book about a frog prince?"

"No. About a frog vampire."

She turns the sketchbook around to show me a picture of a frog with an evil smile and fangs. He's not scary, he's cute—like a little kid dressed up for Halloween. I laugh and say, "That's great!"

Gina laughs, too, and then goes back to sketching.

Hmm . . . I need to make her tell me what her perfect date would be. How do I bring that up? So I say, "Gina? Have you ever thought about writing a book about a girl having a perfect date?"

"Boring! I want to do a book about Frogula!"

"But if you did do that book, the one about the girl, what would her date be like?"

Gina looks up at me and sees that I'm serious. She smiles and says, "Did Scott Dearden ask you out?"

I blush.

Gina pats my arm, leaving fingerprints in colored chalk. "Trust me, Lacey. A good date can be anywhere or anything. All that matters is that there are fireworks. You and Scott could be at the most boring place ever, and if there are fireworks it will be perfect."

Wow, I never would've thought of fireworks. But that's something I can magic up!

Gina closes her sketchbook. "Where are Sunny and Paige? I want to take you Bridemonsters out to dinner."

I rush into the backyard. "Gina wants fireworks!"

Katarina nods. "See, that wasn't so hard, was it?"

"We've got Gina," I say. "Now all we need is Coach Overdale." My heart sinks. "How are we ever going to find him?"

"Bat-n-Putt," Paige says.

"What?"

"That's where Coach Overdale is going to be at seven."

Katarina looks at Paige, surprised. "How do you know that? *Are you a witch?*"

Paige holds up her smartphone. "No, it's on the coach's Facebook page."

Katarina is still mystified. "Is this Facebook a witch?"

When it comes to computers, Katarina is worse than my grandma.

CHAPTER

21

Gina was surprised when we told her that we wanted to have dinner at the Bat-n-Putt. But she said it was our Bridemonster party and we got to choose.

Sunny, Paige, and I get some odd looks as we sit at the outdoor snack bar—it's not every day you see girls in wedding dresses eating chili dogs next to the batting cages. (The chili dogs are *great*. If you're ever around here, you should try them.)

Gina says, "I've never seen you girls eat so slowly."

We're stalling for time waiting for Coach Overdale to show up, so I say, "It's because they're so delicious we want to taste every bite!" We nibble the hot dogs delicately . . .

. . . until Katarina leans down from her gardenia hiding place and whispers, "He's here!"

As the coach walks in from the parking lot, we scarf down everything on our plates in one or two bites—so much for nibbling.

The coach sees us and comes right over, smiling. "Hi, girls. Hi, Gina."

Gina smiles back. "Hi, Brian."

OMG! They know each other's first names. They must have talked when they were trapped together during the frog attack.

Coach Overdale tells me, "I'm glad to see you, Lacey. You're not on my e-mail list yet, and I'm holding an early practice tomorrow morning."

"Okay." Who cares about basketball? It's time for romance. So I tell the coach, "We've never been here before. But Gina wanted to learn how to bat."

Gina says, "Actually . . . I played shortstop in college."

Oh, geez. I even knew that. Did I just wreck everything?

But the coach grins and says, "*I* played shortstop in college! Let's see what you can do!"

And, just like that, Gina and Coach Overdale are in the batting cage together. Paige, Sunny, and I tell them we don't want to get our wedding dresses dirty, so we stand outside watching Gina and the coach hit the balls as they come out of the machine. They're both really good.

When the coach finally misses one, Gina scampers all around him doing a funny victory dance. "I win! I win!"

The coach laughs and pretends to collapse on the ground. Gina pokes him with her bat. "Don't be a quitter! Get up."

Wow. This is the least romantic moment I've ever seen.

But then something cool happens. The coach yanks on the bat and pulls her down to sit next to him. It's not like they're kissing or anything, but they're sitting very, very close.

What they need now is fireworks. Luckily, it's dark enough that we'll be able to see them.

Pointing my wand straight up, I chant, "Fireworks in the sky, like the Fourth of July!"

I know what you're expecting. After the wedding dresses got messed up and the frogs attacked, you think something bad is going to happen with the fireworks. Like they'll burn down the town or make loud farting noises or something.

Well, you're wrong.

The fireworks are *beautiful*.

Blast after blast of sparkles fill the sky—white, pink, blue, and purple. We all turn our faces upward, watching.

At the end, there's a burst of fireworks that forms into red curves. "Look! It's a heart!" Gina says.

The coach looks thoughtful and says, "Maybe it's a sign."

"A sign?"

"That love is in the air."

I hope he'll say more, but he just smiles, gets to his feet, and stretches out his hand to help Gina up. "It was great seeing you again."

"Yes, it was!"

They don't say too much more. But they don't have to. After all—love is in the air.

As Gina drives us home, she's kind of glowing . . . it's more than just fireworks. She says, "That was really fun! Brian is such a nice guy—Lacey, you're lucky to have him for a coach."

In the backseat, both Sunny and Paige give me the thumbs-up (which isn't easy for Paige, since her head is poking out of the sunroof again because of the column).

Here's where I need to be a sneaky fairy godmother and gently push Gina toward the correct decision about getting married. I don't want to say anything too obvious. I *want* to say something subtle, like . . .

"Mom! I think you should marry the coach right away!" Sunny blurts out.

If there was a class in subtle, Sunny would flunk.

Gina blushes and says, "Don't be silly."

Sunny leans forward. "But you like him, don't you?"

"Sure I like him."

"Really, really like him?"

"How could I 'really, really like him' so soon? I just met him today! Don't you think that's a little fast?"

I say, "When you like somebody, you've got to pounce. You're not getting any younger." (I thought that was a good point, but

Katarina groans from behind my gardenias and kicks me in the head.)

Gina laughs. "You're right, he's my last chance. Everybody, hang on. I'm turning this Hyundai around and taking him ring shopping right now."

OMG! *"Really?"*

"No." Gina gives us all a smile. "I know you girls have been worried about me, but I'm going to be just fine, even if I never get married again."

If she only knew what's in store for her!

Katarina and I watch my bedroom clock as the seconds tick down to midnight. At twelve sharp, my wedding dress sparkles away, leaving me in my jeans and T-shirt. When I get married, my dress is going to be a miniskirt with absolutely no train.

As I change into my pajamas, I tell Katarina, "So, I know Gina and the coach are meant to be together. I could tell they really like each other—tonight, they never stopped smiling!"

"All right, fairy godmother, what do you do now?"

"I—I—I don't have enough time! How do I get them from smiling to married?"

"Hints are one thing, but I refuse to just give you the answers. It's your job to figure that out."

I get into bed, still thinking. "I'll have to use a love spell. There's no other way!"

"No! This wedding has to be *true* love, and it has to last! Love spells vanish at midnight, just like your dress did."

"But they would still be married. . . ."

"And unhappy and confused and making plans for a quickie divorce."

I turn off the light, but I don't go to sleep. How am I going to make this work?

CHAPTER
22

The next morning at breakfast, I'm *still* thinking about Gina as I eat my oatmeal. (Katarina's well hidden on top of the refrigerator, crunching on a coffee bean.)

Julius winds around my legs, purring. He purrs even louder as I get up and pop open a can of food for him.

"Lacey, you've already fed him," Mom says.

Oh, right. I already have. My fairy-godmother problems are filling up so much of my brain that there's not even room left over for cat food. But Julius looks so hopeful about getting a double helping that I give it to him anyway. At least I can make *somebody* happy.

As I sit back down, Mom asks me, "What's up with you? Anything you want to talk about?"

I wish I *could* talk to Mom about Gina. And then I realize that maybe I can. So I say, "Why do people get married fast?"

"Fast?"

"Like, in love one day and married the next."

"That never happens!"

"If it did, how would it work?"

"What is this all about?"

"I'm writing a story for English."

"Well . . . if there was a war and one of them was leaving the next day, I guess it could happen."

"There's no war in my story."

"What if someone was going to inherit a fortune, but only if he got married?"

"There's no fortune."

Mom thinks some more. "This is kind of hard, isn't it?"

"Yes!"

Dad shuffles in and listens as he pours himself a cup of coffee.

Mom says, "Green card! What if the girl is from Canada and she's going to be deported unless she marries the boy?"

"Nobody's from Canada. At least, I don't think so."

Mom explains to Dad, "Lacey's writing a story about a girl who needs to get married fast."

Dad sips some coffee. "Maybe she needs to wait to get married. Until she's thirty and has several grad school degrees and she's met a man her father likes and approves of."

Madison skips in, a Barbie in one hand and an Aladdin doll in the other. "Barbie's father didn't approve, but she married Aladdin anyway. And they only met yesterday."

I say, "Madison, this is a grown-up conversation!"

"But you said you wanted to know why people get married fast!"

Madison has ears like a bat—she can hear me tearing open a Snickers bar from anywhere in the house. I say, "Okay, why did Barbie marry Aladdin?"

Madison holds up the dolls. "Barbie told Aladdin that she was getting married to Ken, and that made Aladdin mad. So Aladdin said, 'Barbie, Barbie, marry me right now! Because I loooooove you!'" Madison crams Barbie and Aladdin's faces into each other and makes them kiss.

Dad says, "You know, Barbie doesn't have to get married at all. At least, not till she graduates from medical school."

Madison says, "Dad! Barbie's already a doctor! I have the clothes!" And she makes Barbie and Aladdin kiss some more. If I were Barbie's fairy godmother, I could get her married tomorrow, no problem.

I think some more about why Barbie married Aladdin so fast—it was because Aladdin was jealous and wanted her for himself. When a girl's in demand, you've got to move fast.

Would that work with the coach? Making him jealous? It's worth a try.

When I get to the school parking lot, Katarina looks up at me from inside my pocket. "You're going to do *what*?"

"I'm going to make the coach think Gina's about to marry someone else, to make him jealous."

"How, exactly?"

"I'm going to find him in his office and say, "Coach! Did you hear the exciting news! Gina is getting married to the mayor!"

Katarina shakes her head. "No. Too easy for him to check. Tell him, 'Gina has been pen pals with the czar of Russia, and now the czar's sent for her.'"

"All the czars have been dead for a hundred years."

"Oh! No wonder my Christmas cards keep getting sent back."

I remember Dad pouring himself a cup of coffee this morning. "What if I say, 'Gina is getting married to a Brazilian coffee billionaire. Tomorrow! There's going to be a Frappuccino fountain at the reception!'"

Katarina nods enthusiastically. "Mmmm . . . a Frappuccino fountain!"

We're about to go into the school when Coach Overdale's Mustang pulls in to the parking lot. As I walk toward the car, I see the coach looking at his cell phone. Wait a minute—it's not his cell phone. It's a small, square box, and the lid is open.

And it's not just any box, it's a ring box. With a ring in it. A shiny, sparkly, beautiful, diamond ring! I let out a squeal. OMG! OMG! I don't *have* to make him jealous—he's already one great big step ahead of me. Last night, the coach said, "Love is in the air." And he meant it! He really meant it!

The coach hears my squeal (who wouldn't?), finally sees me, and blushes. Katarina ducks deep inside my pocket as he rolls down the car window.

I say, "That's an engagement ring!"

"It sure is, but you can't tell anyone. I haven't asked Gina yet."

I can't help it; I squeal again. Even Katarina squeals, from inside my pocket. I ask, "Did you decide during the fireworks?"

"Yes. I realized there's only one woman for me."

"How did you find a ring so fast?"

"This was my grandmother's." The coach looks at the ring, smiling.

"When are you going to ask her?"

"Tonight." He snaps the ring box shut and looks at me again, all business. "Remember, not a word about the ring to anybody. And you need to suit up for practice."

"Practice?"

"I told you about it last night, remember? Get changed!" He locks his car and heads for the school.

OMG! OMG! OMG! Getting the coach to propose was amazingly easy, like something out of a fairy tale. It was almost *too* easy. But then I remind myself that fairy tales are never that complicated. Maybe this is just the way it's supposed to be. And with the dress all picked out, the only things I need to worry about are the church and flowers and minister. And a cool party after the wedding. (Hmmm . . . that sounds like a lot. But the proposal was the really, really hard part.)

Katarina pokes her head out of my pocket, a big smile on her face. "I don't know how you did it, Lacey, but you did it!" She opens her notebook, and I see her drawing a star, which fills in with gold the second she finishes the black outline. "Of course, you've got a lot more work to do, but this will look excellent in my report to the Godmother Academy."

Oh, geez: the Academy. I haven't been thinking about it, but that's what all my work is leading to, isn't it? Either that or everyone in the whole world hating me. Neither one of those is my idea of a gold star.

CHAPTER 23

Coach Overdale and the boys on the team groan when Scott throws me a basketball and I drop it.

Scott, who's been demoted from player to equipment manager, just throws me another ball and gives me an encouraging smile. "Come on, Lacey! You're going to be great!"

But I'm *not* going to be great. The only reason I was great before was because I put a spell on myself, and I'm not going to do that anymore. It's not fair, and I don't have time to be on the basketball team!

I throw the ball—and hit the coach right smack on the head.

"Ow!" the coach says.

And I keep being not great for the rest of practice. I'm not great at dribbling, at passing, at shooting, or at free throws. All I'm great at is hitting people on the head.

The coach blows his whistle. "Lacey, we're not playing Whac-A-Mole here! The object of the game is to make a basket, not kill your teammates!" He blows his whistle again. "Everybody, hit the showers."

As the rest of the team heads for the boys' locker room, the coach stops me. "What happened, Lacey? You weren't even trying!"

"I was trying as hard as I could! I'm just a bad player!"

"That's not true. You're fantastic!"

What a joke! "*Please* put Scott back on the team! He deserves it more than me."

The coach looks over at Scott, who's dragging a duffel bag full of basketballs into the equipment room, and says, "Oh, I see what you're doing. You're deliberately playing badly so Scott can get back on the squad."

"No, I'm playing badly because I'm bad!"

"Scott will still like you if you're good at sports. I hate it when girls pretend they're not good at something so boys will like them. You're playing in that game tomorrow, and I'm not changing my mind."

The coach leaves, and Katarina flits down from the rafters. "I thought you played very well. You hit more people on the head than anyone else."

That's me. The hit-the-people-on-the-head girl.

In homeroom, when I tell Sunny about the coach's engagement ring, she squeals even louder than I did. All the kids stare, so I tell them, "She just found out we're having pizza for lunch."

Sunny leans forward and whispers, "You're a *great* fairy godmother! My mom is so lucky! And she's going to be so happy!"

"She's not married yet. We haven't decided anything about the wedding."

"Sure we have! We've got a groom, and a ring, and we even know which dress my mom likes: Paige's Greek one, just without the column."

"We don't have a minister, a cake, flowers, or even a place for the ceremony!" I say. I feel like no matter what I do, there's still more left. And I just have one more day.

Katarina sticks her head out of my pocket, and for once she agrees with me: "It's supposed to be a *dream* wedding—and you haven't done anything about the dream part!"

Sunny crinkles her forehead. "Can we get everything done over lunch and after school?"

"Yes!" Then I think about it. "Maybe." Then I think about it some more, and I crinkle my forehead, too.

Sunny shakes her head. "There's no way we can get it done."

I bet no one in the history of the world ever had to be a fairy godmother and a full-time sixth-grader at the same time. I tell Sunny, "What we need is a snow day."

"Can you make it snow?"

"I think so . . . but if I make a blizzard by mistake, we're not going to get much wedding-planning done."

"A blizzard would be cool. But you're right."

How do you make a snow day without making it snow? This school *never* gets shut down.

Right then, there's a horrible screechy sound from the front of the room—Mrs. Neff, the homeroom teacher, is writing out next week's block schedule on the chalkboard. (She's retiring next year and refuses to switch over to the whiteboard. She says markers smell.) Her chalk screeches again, and Sunny and I both shudder.

I tell Sunny, "I *hate* that sound."

Sunny says, "*Everyone* hates that sound."

Hmmm . . . a sound everyone hates. Could I use that to get the school shut down? I make up a spell and aim my wand at the loudspeaker in the ceiling. I chant, "Out of the speakers come horrible squeakers," and toss the spell.

Screech!

Screech!

SCREECH! the loudspeaker blares, sounding just as horrible as I had hoped it would.

All the kids in the room clap their hands over their ears—and so does Mrs. Neff.

———

Ten minutes later, there are hundreds of kids outside the school. The noise is fainter out here, but we can still hear screechy sounds blasting out of every loudspeaker in every classroom.

Paige runs up to Sunny and me. "Lacey, why?"

(I like how she assumes that anything weird going on is because of me. Aliens could invade tonight and Paige would just think, What's Lacey up to now? and go back to sleep. On the other hand, she happens to be right.)

Sunny tells her, "Lacey's making a snow day. We need to work on the wedding."

Paige nods. "Smart."

Principal Nazarino raises her hands to get our attention. "School is canceled until tomorrow morning. Everyone, go home, now!"

The kids cheer.

CHAPTER 24

I call Mom and tell her school's canceled because the PA system is going crazy. She says it's okay if we go window-shopping in town.

We head straight to the bakery on Walnut Street to pick out the wedding cake—or at least to pick out the kind I'm going to copy tomorrow by magic.

As we peer at the rows of cakes and cupcakes, Sunny says, "At least we know it shouldn't be lemon with buttercream frosting—my mom never wants to eat that again."

But that leaves us with a lot of other choices: red velvet cake, carrot cake, spice cake, coconut cake (yuck!), and banana nut cake. I say, "Everybody, pick one and say it out loud at the same time."

We all look at each other as I count "three, two, one" on my fingers. Then we all say, "CHOCOLATE!"

Well, that was easier than I thought. We pool our money and buy one of the chocolate cupcakes to split. For a moment, we just sit in the bakery enjoying the creamy chocolate icing and the sweet-but-not-too-sweet cake. Cupcakes and friends. What could be better than that? This makes me wonder: will I have cupcakes at the Godmother Academy? Will I even have *friends*?

I know one thing—they won't be as good as the friends I've got right now. I raise my water glass and make a toast: "I love you guys. Let's always remember how happy we are this very second!"

Sunny and Paige smile and clink glasses with me.

Inside my pocket, Katarina gives me a kick and whispers, "Where's *my* cupcake!"

I break off a tiny piece and hand it to her.

"Mmmhmmffmmm!" she says with her mouth full of cake. (Translation: *yummy*.)

"All right, we'll have chocolate cake," I tell the girls. "What else do we need to decide about? I can make flowers by magic. . . ."

"Do we even know what time the wedding's going to be?" Paige asks me.

"The moon is officially full at 9:23 p.m., so the wedding needs to be over by then."

"Can we start at seven?" Sunny asks. "Mom thinks evening weddings are the nicest. Seven is when my mom wanted to get married to Dwight, until he said City Hall."

Paige shakes her head. "That's when the basketball game starts, and I'm cheering."

Oh, right. The coach will need to be there, too, and I'm supposed to play in the game. Well, *that's* not going to happen. I still want the game to go on, but it's not fair for me to play using my magic powers. And without magic powers, all I'd do is make the team lose.

I ask Sunny, "Do you think five o'clock is okay? That's *almost* evening."

When Sunny nods, I say, "Okay! So that leaves us with two big things: who's going to perform the ceremony, and where the wedding's going to be. I wonder what spell I should use to make a minister?"

"No spells for the minister," Katarina pipes up from my pocket. "If you want the wedding to be real, you need a real minister. A lot of other things can be magic, but not that."

Hmmm. . . . *This* could be a problem. But then I think of something that might just solve everything. "The coach is going to ask Gina to marry him tonight, right? After she says yes, we'll run in and tell them they've won a dream wedding."

Paige says, "Like in a contest or something?"

"Yes, a big contest where the wedding has to be tomorrow. And we'll let Gina and the coach figure out the minister. We're doing everything else—they can at least do that much."

Under the table, I cross my fingers.

The woman who owns the bakery brings us three more chocolate cupcakes, then gives me a wink. "These are on the house. I saw you putting the crumbs into your pocket, and anyone who likes my desserts that much deserves seconds."

We all say thank you and dive in. "Save *me* some," Katarina says. "You wouldn't even have those cupcakes if it weren't for me!"

Paige hands Katarina a little piece, then says with a smile, "Maybe we should hold the ceremony right here."

My mouth suddenly feels really dry. "Where *are* we going to hold the ceremony?"

We spend the rest of the afternoon biking all over town, searching.

We try the obvious places. We knock on the door of every church and every banquet hall—but they're already booked for Friday night. Some of them won't even be available for a whole year!

When there's no door left to knock on, we end up back at Fountain Park. It's the only place I can think of to hold the wedding ceremony.

Paige says, "It's so depressing here! Lacey, do you think you can make this place look good enough for a wedding?"

"Well, let's find out." I pull my wand out of my pocket and chant, "The fountain oughter look better with water."

Katarina cringes. "That's a horrible rhyme!"

Horrible or not, the rhyme works, and the fountain fills to the brim. We all jump away when water sprays into the air, but it lands perfectly back in the fountain and even makes a double rainbow.

"What else?" I ask.

Sunny says, "Flowers!"

"Grass!" Paige says.

"A rhyme that doesn't stink," Katarina says. "Take some pride in your work!"

I chant, "There's no April showers, but we need grass and flowers."

Katarina says, "Better. Not great. But it doesn't make me want to vomit."

I wave my wand all around the park. The dry dirt sprouts lush, green grass. And every bush and tree puts out white and pink blossoms, perfect for a wedding.

Sunny flops down on the grass. "This place is *great!* I wish they could get married right this minute!"

I look around at the beautiful park. Every single thing for the wedding is falling into place.

So why do I feel so nervous?

CHAPTER

25

After the park, we go to Sunny's house to wait for Coach Overdale to show up and propose to Gina. She'll be so surprised when her prince rides up on his white horse. Okay, there probably won't be a white horse, but the coach does drive a white Mustang.

As soon as we go inside, Sunny yells, "Mom! We're home!"

We find Gina at her drawing table working on more Frogula sketches.

"Great timing, girls. I'm done for the day," Gina says, standing up and tugging at her wrinkled T-shirt and torn yoga pants. "What's up?"

Katarina whispers to me, "That definitely doesn't look like a woman who's about to get a proposal—unless the proposal is to take those clothes and burn them."

Gina does need to be spruced up before Coach Overdale arrives. I think about zapping her the way I did at the emergency room, but this time I think she'd notice. Instead, I tell her, "We wanted to do beauty makeovers. Can you help?"

Gina *loves* this idea. "How fun!"

So, for the next couple of hours, we all put on makeup and lipstick, curl our hair, and polish our nails. (I almost forgot about the nails part, but Katarina whispers that chipped nails are tacky when the prince puts the ring on, even if the prince is just a basketball coach.) When we're done, Gina looks amazing. She's changed into a cashmere sweater with a skirt and high heels, and her shining hair curls around her shoulders. And she's wearing just enough makeup to look like she's not wearing makeup at all.

I keep looking out the window, hoping the coach will show up. But none of the cars that drive by are his Mustang.

Where is he?

Then my cell phone rings—it's Mom, wanting me to come to the Hungry Moose *right now.* I try to argue, but when Mom says, "right now," in that tone, it means right *now.*

I tell Sunny, "I've got to go. But text me the second Coach shows up."

"Will do."

"Paige, do you want to come with me to the restaurant?"

"No. I'm meeting my dad at the hospital cafeteria for dinner."

I check the driveway one more time, but there's no white Mustang.

Hurry up, Coach! You're getting married tomorrow!

When I walk into the kitchen at the Hungry Moose, I'm a little worried that Mom's mad at me. She doesn't "right now" me all that often.

Mom's not mad, but she's definitely not smiling. "There you are, Lacey! You promised to alphabetize the spices in the storeroom."

Oops. I did promise, last week. But that seems so long ago now. I walk into the big, windowless storeroom, wondering who's going to sort Mom's spices when I go to the Academy. I'm the only one who likes to do it.

I flip on the light—and in the middle of the worktable, there's a new satin basketball uniform in purple and gold, the school colors.

"Surprise!" Mom, Dad, and Madison shout behind me. Everybody gives me a big hug. (Nobody except me hears the little *oof* in my pocket when Katarina gets squished.)

"We rush-ordered your uniform," Mom says. "Aren't you excited it's here?"

"It's sooooo pretty!" Madison says.

Oh, geez. I've been thinking about the wedding so much that I keep forgetting about basketball.

Dad tells me, "For the game tomorrow, I'm going to shut the restaurant early. I haven't done that since Madison was born."

They all look so happy and excited—but I've got a wedding to plan! I say, "Uh . . . I'm not really sure I even *want* to play."

Dad says, "Of course you do! When I was playing football I was always scared the night before a game, just like you." He kisses me on the forehead. "I don't want you to ever forget how proud of you I am."

He looks happy. Really, really happy.

I'm *not* playing in the game—but now, for the first time, I'm picturing Dad showing up at the gym tomorrow and me not being there. He'll be so disappointed! And the last thing I want to do is disappoint my dad. Or Mom. Or Madison.

Wedding, basketball, Academy. My mind is going around in circles.

All evening I sit with Madison as she makes glitter-covered macaroni necklaces to wear to the game tomorrow night. She talks me into helping. At least it's something for me to do when I'm not texting Sunny.

Me, 7:16 p.m.: *Is he there yet?*

Sunny, 7:17 p.m.: *No.*

Me, 8:04 p.m.: *Any sign?*

Sunny, 8:05 p.m.: *No!*

Me, 8:42 p.m.: *He must be there!*

Sunny, 8:43 p.m.: *NOOOO!!! He's not!*

Finally it's time for the restaurant to close. Dad finishes cleaning the grill, and Mom turns out the lights. "Come on, everybody! Let's go home!"

The second we get home, I text Sunny again.

Me, 9:37 p.m.: *Where is he?*

Sunny, 9:38 p.m.: *I don't know!*

Katarina reads Sunny's text over my shoulder and says, "Maybe he got eaten by trolls."

"That happens?"

"Certainly. A troll ate one of my best friends."

I sigh. "As if I needed more to worry about. I'm already worried about Dad being disappointed in me. I'm worried about the wedding. And I'm worried about going away to a fairy school for a hundred years."

"The wedding is the only thing you need to concern yourself with now. You are a fairy-godmother-in-training. And tomorrow is the most important test of your life."

"But tomorrow could be the last time I see my family."

"You're still fussing about that?" Katarina says, truly surprised. She just doesn't get it.

"Yes, I'm still fussing! Do I *have* to go away to the Academy?"

"Yes."

"What if I do the wedding—and then run away?"

"They'd find you. They're fairy godmothers, remember?" Katarina darts over, perches on my shoulder, and gives me a little pat of encouragement. "You're going to love the Academy!"

My phone pings with a text. I pick it up, feeling hopeful— the coach must finally be there!

But the text from Sunny only says, *My mom is putting on her pajamas. What do I do?*

I text back, *Keep her awake.*

Sunny texts, *I'll try.*

I sit on the bed, chewing what's left of my nails. I close my eyes for half a second . . .

. . . and when I open them, there's a bright light shining in through my window, as if somebody turned on a spotlight.

OMG!

It's not a spotlight—it's the sun! I must have fallen asleep!

I check the clock—it's 7:18 a.m. That can't be right! I look at my phone to double-check. The clock's not right. It's actually 7:19!

Why didn't Katarina wake me up? Then I hear her snoring on my dresser. She fell asleep, too.

I jab out a text on my phone: *Did he propose?*

A moment or two later, Sunny texts back: *He never even showed up.*

Noooooooooooo!!!!!

CHAPTER 26

'm dressed and out of the house in five minutes flat. A new record.

When I get to school, there's nobody around yet. I hurry down the empty hall so fast that Katarina has to flutter extra hard to keep up. "The clock is ticking," she huffs. "If Gina isn't happily married by 9:23 tonight, every person on earth will hate you!"

"Maybe you should have thought of that when you let me fall asleep."

"I didn't let you fall asleep. You let *me* fall asleep." Katarina disappears into my pocket as if that settles the argument.

I reach the coach's office and find him sitting in his chair, drinking coffee and looking like the most depressed man in the world.

"Hi, Coach," I say.

"Practice starts in fifteen minutes. I'll be right out." He slumps even further down in his chair.

I decide the blunt approach is best. "Did you ask Gina to marry you, like you said?"

"I don't want to talk about it."

"People feel better when they talk about things—at least, that's what my mom says. *Did* you ask Gina?"

He sighs. "I never even got the chance. I went to her house, but she wouldn't open the door. She said it was too late and that I was clueless."

Wow, once Gina's in her pajamas, visiting hours are over. And he was soooo close.

I tell him, "You need to go ask her right now, this morning!" I walk around the desk and try to pull him out of his chair. "What are you waiting for? You've got the ring. You've got somebody to propose to. So, *propose!*"

But the coach won't budge. He's like Julius when he doesn't want to get off my bed—suddenly he weighs ten times more than he did before. "Lacey, get out of my office. When you're a grown-up, you'll understand how complicated things can be sometimes."

He thinks *I* don't understand how complicated things can be? He's got no idea. "Please, Coach. Now's your big chance! Go ask Gina to marry you!"

"Lacey, I've been polite. But GO!"

As I back out of the office into the hallway, Katarina pokes her head out of my pocket, looking thoughtful.

"Katarina, what do I do?"

"Finding a prince usually isn't so hard."

"But we found the prince! He just won't propose! So what do I do now?"

"To be honest, I don't know."

"You've got to know! How do I make the coach propose to Gina?"

"I don't think you can."

I feel like throwing myself on the floor and having a tantrum. The fairy godmothers gave me a test that nobody could pass. I *hate* fairy godmothers!

It's all so stupid. We were so close—the coach was on Gina's porch last night with a ring. And he couldn't ask her, because she's a morning person.

Wait a minute.

He still wants to marry her; he's just being stubborn about it. What he needs right now is a little push.

A little, tiny push. I murmur, "What rhymes with *Gina*?"

"Lacey, no! It has to be true love."

"It *is* true love. It just needs to be fast!"

All the rhymes are bad. *Nina* and *Lena* and *Argentina* and even *Katarina*. Then it hits me! I go back to the doorway of the coach's office, pull out my wand, and chant, "You'll never love another, so propose to Sunny's mother!"

In my pocket, Katarina punches me with her little fists. I know how *she* feels about what I'm doing.

When I toss the spell at the coach, he closes his eyes for a second like he's hearing sweet music. He smiles a goofy smile, and when his eyes flutter back open, they're smiling, too. He leaps from his chair and shouts, "I'M GOING TO GET MARRIED!"

I nod. "You're going to get married today at five!"

"I'M GOING TO GET MARRIED TODAY AT FIVE!" he shouts. He pushes past me and runs into the hall.

I scurry after him, and we pass by the door of the gym, where the boys on the basketball team are waiting.

Scott says, "The door's still locked, Coach!"

"And it can stay locked. Boys, let me share some advice. Basketball doesn't matter. Work doesn't matter. All that matters is LOVE!"

He shouts so loud that Principal Nazarino pokes her head out of her office at the far end of the hall to see what's going on.

Scott says, "But the game—"

"The game is canceled! Be like me, boys. Go find yourselves somebody to propose to, today!"

Wow, that proposal spell really, really worked! The boys gawk as he skips away.

Scott calls after him, "We can't cancel the game—it's the first one."

And Dylan Hernandez shouts, "We'll be *losers*!"

The coach doesn't look back. He tells Principal Nazarino, "Wish me luck. I'm going to propose to Sunny's mother."

Her eyes open wide—that's not something a principal expects one of her teachers to tell her. When the coach is gone, she goes back inside her office and slams the door so hard it almost falls off the hinges. Geez. I hope I didn't just get the coach fired.

The boys on the team look shocked. You'd think the coach had canceled the whole season, not just the first game.

I turn to Scott. "*You* coach them today."

"I'm not the coach."

"But you're good with people; you helped me. And you can use Coach's playbook."

"We can't even get into the gym!"

Well, *that's* not a big deal. I hide the wand in my hand, aim it at the lock, and whisper, "On count of four, open the door. One, two, three, *four*." There's a little clicking sound, and I turn the knob. "See? It wasn't locked at all. You guys go in and practice."

The boys go into the gym, but Scott sees me starting to leave. "We need you, too, Lacey."

"No, you don't. You've got the whole team."

"But you're the best! Everybody knows it."

"I'm not good at all. I was just having a lucky day or two." (If you can call a magic spell luck.)

"Lacey, we need you. *I* need you. Please stay."

Scott stares at me like a puppy with the world's longest eyelashes.

"Well . . . I have to go right now, but I'll see you at the game."

"You promise?"

I *can't* promise. I don't want to use magic to cheat at basketball anymore, and without magic, I'm still a sucky player.

Scott keeps staring at me hopefully. Oh, *geez.*

Well . . . the wedding's at five. The game's at seven. If I'm *not* sucky, maybe I can do both. Maybe a little . . . magic wouldn't be so bad. Would it?

I tell Scott, "Yes, I'll be there."

When I reach the parking lot, the coach is just pulling out, going so fast his tires are screeching. I text Sunny and Paige: *He's on his way to propose!*

Yay!

Katarina emerges from my pocket and hovers near my head. "This is going to be a total disaster."

CHAPTER 27

As I walk to Sunny's house, Katarina flies alongside me complaining about what a botch I've made of things.

Finally I can't take it anymore. "If you can't say something helpful, don't say anything at all."

She pretends to lock her lips shut and throw away the key. But even without words, I can tell she's *still* complaining.

When we reach the house, Paige and Sunny are standing on the porch. I run up to them, excited. "Is the coach inside? Is he proposing?"

Sunny shakes her head. *"He's not here.* This is going to be just like last night—he's not going to show up!"

I say, "Actually, he was here last night. He said he knocked and Gina wouldn't even open the door, because it was too late."

Sunny says, "But I would have heard that!"

This is so confusing! What happened last night? Sunny's acting like the coach didn't come to her house at all—but he said he did! Then I figure it out and ask Sunny, "Were you asleep?"

"Maybe."

"That explains it. You know you can sleep through anything!" Which is true. To get out of bed every morning, Sunny needs two alarm clocks plus her mom. "He must have been here and you didn't even wake up."

But where's the coach right now? He was doing a hundred miles an hour out of the parking lot. He should have been here way before me.

Paige sees him first. "There he is!"

Katarina sighs loudly and flies back into my pocket.

Coach Overdale parks at the curb, and there's a kid in the passenger seat—it's Martin Shembly, the boy who played the *Star Trek* theme song at the mascot competition. *That's* strange.

When the coach gets out of the car, I see he's changed into a suit and tie. He gives us a cheery wave. "Hi, girls! What a *beautiful* morning for a proposal! I'm head over heels!" He does a cartwheel on the lawn.

Paige looks at me, shocked. "You put a spell on him?"

Katarina hisses up at her, "I told her not to!"

I say, "I had to hurry things up! He had the ring, and he wanted to propose, so I nudged him a little."

When the coach does another cartwheel, Paige says, "You nudged him a *lot*!"

The coach pulls a folding table out of his trunk and sets it up on the front lawn. He adds a white linen tablecloth, a couple of candlesticks, and a vase containing a single rose.

While the coach is smoothing out the creases in the tablecloth, I walk over to Martin. "What are you doing here?"

"The coach said he'd get me out of PE for the rest of the year if I helped him."

"Helped him how?"

The coach snaps his fingers. "Martin! Set the mood!"

Martin takes his violin out of the backseat and starts to play—I don't know the song, but whatever it is, it's romantic.

As Martin plays, the coach grabs a champagne bottle and two glasses from the trunk and puts them on the table. He nods, satisfied. Then he walks up to the door and knocks.

Here comes the proposal!

I'm not going to say I'm the best fairy godmother ever . . .

. . . but I am! I'm the best fairy godmother ever! In less than a week, I've found Gina the perfect husband, and now he's proposing! This is *awesome*!

Gina opens the door. "Brian? What are you doing here?"

"Come with me." He puts out his hand and she hesitates—
this has to be pretty strange for her. Then she sees me, Sunny,
and Paige smiling and giggling, and she relaxes.

Gina takes Coach Overdale's hand, and he leads her to the
little table on the lawn as Martin plays romantic music. The
coach pulls out a chair. "Please, darling, sit."

She sits, but she also frowns. "What's all this about?"

When the coach gets down on one knee, Gina frowns even
harder. "This isn't funny."

Because of the love spell, the coach smiles at her as if she had just said, "OH MY GOSH!" like all the women in movies and TV commercials always do. He gazes lovingly into her eyes and says, "Sunny's mother, will you marry me?"

She stiffens. "Are you insane? Brian, I don't know what you're doing, but stop it! I'm going to go inside and pretend this never happened."

"You must not have heard me. Sunny's mother—marry me! Today, at five p.m.!"

She jumps up so fast she knocks over her chair.

"Sunny's mother! What are you doing?"

Paige whispers to me, "Why does he keep calling her that?"

"It was in the spell—nothing rhymed with *Gina.*"

Gina runs into the house and slams the door. The coach follows her and rings the bell. "Sunny's mother? Please come out and marry me. Sunny's mother? Don't destroy all that we've built together!"

Gina opens the door: "We've known each other for precisely two days! We haven't built anything! GO AWAY!"

"MARRRRY MEEEEEEEE!"

"I'm calling the police!"

She slams the door again, and the coach collapses on the doorstep, sobbing.

Martin stops playing romantic music. "I still get out of PE, right?"

The coach nods yes and cries some more.

Martin smiles and starts playing a funeral march to go along with the coach's tears.

Katarina whispers up at me from my pocket, "I suggest you do something before Gina really does call the police."

Yikes! She's right!

I motion to the girls, and we all run behind the house, where Fifi the poodle barks at us like we're burglars.

We go in through the sliding glass door and find Gina picking up the phone.

"Gina, wait!" I say. "I know you're confused about why Coach Overdale is proposing to you right now. But I can explain everything!"

The girls stare at me, and then Katarina murmurs, "This had better be good!"

I start with the truth: "Coach Overdale is in love with you, and he wants to give you his grandmother's ring and marry you."

"He can give me rings from everyone in his family, but I'm not going to marry him!"

"But you *like* him."

"Sure, I like him. But he's *crazy*. And crazy's a deal-breaker!"

"He's not crazy. He's crazy in love!"

On the front lawn, the coach starts singing, "Sunny's mother, I love you!"

Gina listens for a second, and then says, "No, he's just crazy crazy."

I need to try another approach. "He only seems crazy because the proposal was so sudden. But what if you had dated him . . . if you had met his family . . . if he had given you flowers on your birthday . . . Would you marry him then?"

Gina hesitates. "Maybe. But that didn't happen, did it?"

She said *maybe*, and that means that if the godmothers gave me a year and not a week, I could get Gina her dream wedding, no problem. But I don't have a year. I only have until 9:23 this evening!

I *know* that for Gina to get her dream, it has to be true love. But, I keep telling myself, this *is* true love—I did the love-locator test! What more proof do I need?

None.

I hate to do what I'm about to do, but this is the only way. So nervous that my hand shakes, I raise my wand and chant, "Love must prevail, so marry Coach Overdale."

I'm about to toss the spell when Katarina flings herself onto the wand and tries to yank it away from me. "Lacey! No!"

Gina looks at Katarina, agog. "What is that?"

Oops.

I manage to flick Katarina away, and I toss the spell right at Gina. She blinks as if a bright camera flash just went off, then smiles. Her smile is even goofier than the coach's.

"Now you've done it!" Katarina shouts.

Sunny and Paige look at me, confused. I say, "Gina's not going to be happy unless she gets married today. I had to use a spell."

Katarina slowly shakes her head. "Lacey, you'll go down in the history books as the worst fairy-godmother candidate ever. Even worse than—"

I'm actually a little curious to find out who the next-worst candidate is, but before Katarina has a chance to finish, Gina rushes to the front door, flings it open, and runs outside. "Coach Overdale! I LOVE YOU!"

The coach hugs her. "Sunny's mother! I LOVE YOU!"

I wish they would use first names—it would be nicer, don't you think?

They gaze into each other's eyes, totally love-struck. Then the coach gets down on one knee and takes the ring out of his pocket. He says, "Sunny's mother—will you marry me today at five?"

Gina says, "Yes, Coach Overdale. I *will* marry you today at five!"

Sunny, Paige, Katarina, and I watch from the front door as the coach slips the ring on Gina's finger. Then they kiss. I know this is happening because of a magic spell, but it's still really,

really romantic. When Martin starts playing the violin, it's like the best perfume commercial ever.

Gina and the coach really *do* seem to belong together. Maybe I did cheat, a smidge. Well, a lot. But I had to! And look how well it's working out!

The kiss goes on and on, and Sunny finally tugs on Gina's sleeve. "*Mom!* This is embarrassing!"

Gina stops kissing the coach long enough to tell Sunny, "It's not embarrassing, it's love!"

"And you're happy?"

"Of course I am! Who *wouldn't* be happy marrying Coach Overdale today at five?"

The coach kisses Gina again. "Oh, darling!" he cries.

"Oh, darling!" Gina replies.

Oh, puke! They're acting like Aladdin and Barbie when Madison was mushing them together. This *is* embarrassing. Plus, we're never going to get anything done if they keep kissing all day.

I tell Martin, "Good job! Homeroom's in fifteen minutes. You'd better go."

Martin looks happy not to have to watch any more kissing. He packs up his violin and hurries away.

Then I shout, "GINA! COACH! TIME OUT!" They stop kissing for a moment and look at me, surprised. Now what do I do with them? It's a long time till the wedding.

I'm about to lock the coach in the garage when I remember something: we need to find a real, nonmagical minister. Maybe I can put the coach to work.

So I say, "Coach, you're the groom. And everyone knows the groom isn't supposed to see the bride before the wedding; it's bad luck. Do you understand?"

The coach nods.

"I'm going to give you a very important job. You need to go out and find a minister, or there won't be any wedding at all. And you don't want that, do you?"

"No! My heart would stop beating, and I would cry a million tears."

(I don't think you can cry even one tear if your heart isn't beating. Does love make you stupid?)

Gina tells him, "And I would cry *two* million tears."

(Yep, love makes you stupid.)

Before they start smooching again, I push the coach toward his car. "Go find us a minister in time for the wedding! And drive carefully!"

The coach runs to his car and then stops. What now? He asks me, "Where *is* the wedding?"

Good question. I'm about to tell him to go to Fountain Park, but then I remember the basketball game. How will I get to the game in time? I promised Scott I'd be there. This just gets more and more complicated! It would sure be easier to have the wedding and the game closer to each other.

I make a snap decision and tell the coach, "Meet us at the school cafeteria."

"Cafeteria! Got it!" He gets into his car and drives off.

Sunny stares at me. "The *cafeteria*?"

Paige is equally shocked. *"Gross!"*

Katarina nods. "Gross, indeed."

"I want to play in the basketball game tonight, and Paige needs to cheer, so everything has to be close together. I'll make it nice, trust me."

Gina stands on the sidewalk, waving at the coach's car. "Good-bye, my love! Good-bye!"

Geez, if I'm not careful, she's going to wander off. I think about locking *her* in the garage, but that's not a very nice thing to do to a woman on her wedding day. Most brides spend the whole day with a stylist working on their hair and makeup and nails, not staring at the lawn mower.

As I lean against the fence, trying to figure out what to do, Fifi the poodle runs up from the other side and barks at me. Her rhinestone collar sparkles in the sun, and her pink bow is placed at a jaunty angle. Even though she's a dog, she's the most fashionable person around.

I suddenly know where to get Gina the extra bridal help she

needs. I raise my wand and chant, "A perfect bride needs Fifi at her side."

When I toss the spell at her, Fifi starts to spin around faster and faster.

Then there's a puff of sparkles, and a beautiful woman appears on our side of the fence, dressed in stylish black clothes and spike heels. She's still got the pink bow and rhinestone collar, but even they look classier now. Fifi says, in a strong French accent, "Where is ze bride?"

"Here is ze bride," I say, and point at Gina.

Katarina shakes her head. "Zees will never work."

Gina doesn't seem too surprised to see a strange Frenchwoman standing on the lawn. (When you're goofy from a love spell, not much surprises you.)

"Gina," I say, "this is Fifi. She'll be helping you get ready for the wedding."

Gina smiles dreamily. "It's my wedding day, and I'm so in love!"

Fifi nods. "And we will make you into a beautiful bride. But zose eyebrows! *Sacre bleu!*"

Fifi turns to me and asks, "How long before ze wedding?"

"It's this afternoon."

"We will need every second!" She leads Gina into the house and shuts the door.

Sunny, Paige, and I exchange worried glances—and then we run.

School starts in five minutes!

CHAPTER

28

The bell is ringing when Paige, Sunny, and I skid through the school's front doors. We made it!

Well, actually, we're about twenty seconds late. But who's counting?

Principal Nazarino, that's who. Katarina squeezes deep down into my pocket as the principal marches up to us and yells, "You're late! And do you know what happens when you're late?"

Usually, detention is what happens, but Nazarino seems like she's in an extra bad mood this morning, so it could be anything.

Before we have a chance to find out, the school secretary, Mrs. Fleecy, sticks her head out of the office. "Principal Nazarino! We still haven't found a substitute for Coach Overdale."

The principal snaps, "Girls, get to class instantly!" And she disappears into the office.

Saved!

In my morning classes, all I do is think about the wedding. If this goes on much longer, I'll flunk out of school, for sure.

Later, as I hurry down the hallway to meet Sunny and Paige for lunch, Mr. Griffith stops me. "Lacey Unger-Ware! Just the girl I wanted to see!"

"I am?"

"Yes!"

He looks very serious. "I have some news about the mascot competition. The votes are counted—and it's a tie between the Grizzly and the Bridemonsters. Congratulations on your nomination!"

"Uh . . . thank you."

"Don't thank me—thank your classmates for voting for you! During halftime at tonight's basketball game, there's going to be a runoff. To win, you girls need to bring your dresses and take that Grizzly *down*!"

I thought my life couldn't get any weirder. And yet it just did. Not only do I have to plan a wedding and play in a basketball game that I don't deserve to play in, but now I have to participate in a mascot competition. At least I have a good excuse for why we can't do the runoff. I say, "I'm really sorry, Mr. Griffith, but we don't have the dresses anymore. They got sent back to where they came from."

Mr. Griffith shakes a finger at me. "Don't give me any

excuses. Your peers have given you this wonderful chance, and you can't disappoint them. I don't care if you have to wear a dress made out of your mother's sheets. You *will* be there!"

"But, Mr. Griffith!"

"No buts! Be there!" He walks away.

Whatever Mr. Griffith says, the Bridemonsters will *not* be making a halftime appearance. No way, no how.

Paige and Sunny are waiting for me at a corner table in the cafeteria, and I tell them about the runoff (and how we're not doing it).

Sunny is bummed. "Being the mascot would have been cool. Lacey, you're on the basketball team. And Paige, you're a cheerleader. It would have been something for *me* to do. Can't we try to do it?" She turns to me and says, "You could magic up the wedding dresses again."

I tell her, "I feel bad, but there's just no time. The wedding is way more important."

"You're right." Sunny sighs. "But still . . ."

I take Katarina out of my pocket and hide her behind a milk carton so she can join in with the wedding planning—there's so much noise that nobody but us can hear her.

She peers past the carton into the cafeteria and holds her nose. "It's disgusting in here! And what's that *smell*?"

Sunny says, "Lunch."

Katarina glares at me. "*This* is where you're planning to hold the wedding?"

Paige nods. "I thought the park was depressing, but at least it doesn't smell like tuna-roni and feet."

I ask Katarina, "You don't think the cafeteria will work?"

"I didn't say that. I once transformed a sewer in New Jersey into a lovely, sun-dappled beach."

"Why were you in a sewer?"

"I'm saving that story for my memoirs. But believe me, it smelled better than this place."

I point at the corner next to the soda machines. "The minister can stand there. I'll add a white carpet, roses, and stained-glass windows."

The girls look around, trying to picture where everything will go. I tell them, "Trust me, it'll be great!"

"What'll be great?" Martin Shembly asks, sitting down with his tray. We were so busy imagining the wedding that none of us saw him walk over. Katarina, with no chance to hide, can't do anything but freeze like a statue.

Martin stuffs a fistful of french fries into his mouth and looks right at her. "Awesome action figure!" Before I can stop him, he picks Katarina up and peers at her frozen expression. "The detail is amazing! Look at her mean little face. What universe is she from? Not Narnia. Not Lord of the Rings. Not Harry Potter."

He starts yanking on her hair. "Is her head detachable?"

I reach over and grab her away from him. "No, it's not detachable! You're going to break her. I mean . . . it!" I put Katarina in my pocket and change the subject by telling Martin, "Great violin playing this morning."

Sunny, trying to be helpful, says, "My mom really liked it!"

Martin smiles at her, and I suddenly realize—he's sort of cute. Not Scott Dearden cute, but not a troll, either. He asks Sunny, "So your mom's really going to marry the coach? Tough break!"

Sunny says, "I think he's nice!"

"Yeah, if you like running laps and doing push-ups."

Sunny looks worried—she *hates* push-ups.

But Martin tells her, "You can get out of it. I get out of gym all the time. I learned how to fake a hamstring injury on YouTube."

Sunny says, "Really?"

Martin grabs his leg, groans, and falls off his chair with a thud.

Sunny says, "You're *weird*!"

But she can't help laughing.

I somehow make it through my afternoon classes, no thanks to Katarina, who keeps whispering from my pocket, "Do you think I have a mean face?"

I ignore her the first couple of times, but then she starts

kicking me. "Answer me! Do you think I have a mean face!"

"That's just Martin's opinion."

"I'm not mean! How can he say I'm mean? Next time I see that boy I'm going to put an itching spell on him."

Nope, she's not mean at all.

The last bell finally rings, and I race out into the hall to meet Sunny and Paige at the cafeteria. The kids in the hallway are strangely subdued, especially for a Friday afternoon—nobody's running and shouting or banging their lockers like they usually do.

Sunny and Paige are already waiting for me at the locked cafeteria door. "Why's everyone so quiet?" I ask.

"Principal Nazarino is in the worst mood ever. She's already put ten kids in detention," Sunny says.

I use a spell to unlock the door and get us into the cafeteria before we get put in detention, too.

Now that it's been closed up for a couple of hours, the cafeteria smells worse than ever. To air it out, we swing the back doors open and shut—a lot!—but the tuna-roni-and-feet smell refuses to leave.

Katarina puts on a tiny gas mask. She's exaggerating, but not by much.

"You've got to do something, Lacey," Sunny says.

Think about it—it's a lot harder getting rid of a smell than making it. It's like putting perfume back in a bottle after you've sprayed it.

Actually, with a little magic, putting perfume back in a bottle doesn't sound too tough. Problem: no perfume bottle. I look into the garbage can near the door, and all I see is garbage—kids at Lincoln Middle School don't throw out a lot of Chanel No. 5. Wait, there's an empty Tic Tac container!

I fish it out and pop open the plastic lid. Then I chant, "Bad air is boxed, sealed and locked!" Even though it's not a perfect rhyme, as soon as I toss the spell, the bad air in the room condenses into dark and cloudy wisps. A moment later, all the wisps swirl into the Tic Tac box.

I snap the box shut and cautiously sniff the air. For the first time I can remember, the cafeteria smells clean—like it had never, ever heard of tuna-roni. I throw the Tic Tac box into the trash can. The smells will come back at midnight, but by then we'll all be gone.

Twenty minutes and a lot of zapping later, I've turned the cafeteria into a beautiful wedding chapel. We all stand around admiring the makeover.

Colored light streams in through the stained-glass windows. Beautiful chandeliers flicker with hundreds of white candles (Paige's idea), and daisies, orchids, and roses line the aisle

(Sunny's idea). An arch made out of orange-tree branches fills the space where the soda machine was (my idea). And a huge fire extinguisher sits in the back (Katarina's idea—she says you can never be too careful around candles, especially magic ones).

"This is even better than the park," Sunny says.

With one final zap, the wedding cake appears. It forms itself from the inside out: first, the chocolate filling, all gooey and delicious-looking; then the cake, moist and cocoa brown; and finally, the white-chocolate frosting, with a whole garden of sugary leaves and flowers. I haven't spent all my life watching Dad decorate cakes at the restaurant for nothing.

"We're all set," I say. "Let's go get the bride!"

CHAPTER

29

We leave Paige to stand guard at the cafeteria door (the janitor would have a heart attack if he saw a chapel instead of a lunchroom) and go back to Sunny's house.

Fifi waits for us outside Gina's bedroom. "Finally, you have returned! Ze bride looks *très, très, magnifique!*" She opens the door like she's revealing a precious work of art.

Katarina, Sunny, and I all gasp.

To be fair, Fifi did a wonderful job with Gina's makeup and manicure. Even Gina's toenails have a pink, pearly shine. *But her hair!*

Her hair would be great—if Gina were a poodle! It's been frizzed out in three clumps: a big pouf on top and two little poufs over her ears. Each pouf is separated by a big pink bow.

Any normal bride would be in tears right now, but the love

spell is so strong that Gina can't be anything but happy, no matter what happens. She fluffs her poodle-y hair. "Fifi says I look just like a princess."

"Only if the princess is a dog," Katarina whispers.

Not wanting to hurt Fifi's feelings (and also because I'm a tiny bit afraid she'll bite me), I ask her to get us some tea from the kitchen. When she hesitates, I say, "Fifi! Fetch us tea!" She cheers right up and scampers out of the room.

I close the door, and Sunny says, "Mom's hair isn't going to be like that till midnight, is it?"

"No, it's not a spell. But *this* is." I chant, "Hair horrific, turn terrific!" When I toss the spell, the poodle-pouf horror disappears from Gina's head and is replaced by a smooth, gleaming French twist.

Gina admires herself in the mirror, and says, "This looks nice, too!"

Now it's time for the dress. I picture the one that Paige wore, and work as hard as I can *not* to think of the Greek column that came with it. I chant, "Time for the dress, so we'll have success!"

The fabric of Gina's faded pink bathrobe melts away like popping champagne bubbles. The terry cloth turns into white silk that swirls around before finally settling into a gorgeous wedding gown. There's a magic shimmer to the silk, as if the popping champagne bubbles were part of the fabric.

I peer around at the back of the dress, worried. No Greek column. Phew!

Sunny says, "Mom! You look amazing!"

Gina stares at Sunny, a little glassy-eyed, like she's not quite sure who Sunny even is. But she nods and smiles, then twirls in the dress. The gown sparkles and shimmers, and I have no doubt that she's the most beautiful bride I've ever seen.

Katarina tells me, "Lacey Unger-Ware, you may be below average as a fairy godmother, but you have an unexpected flair for dresses. I'll make a note of that for the Academy."

Sunny says, "Academy? What Academy?"

Katarina says, "She hasn't told you? She's going to—"

I clamp down on Katarina's head with my finger and thumb to make her shut up. "Sunny, it's just something we're talking about. I'll tell you later."

"But I want to know!"

I don't *want* Sunny to know I'm going away. She'll get hysterical, and then I'll get hysterical, and then we'll both be hysterical, which won't do anyone any good.

Katarina pokes my thumb with her magic wand and I let go. She flies to the mirror and angrily fluffs up her hair. "The next person who touches my head gets turned into a tree slug!"

Just then, Fifi comes back with the tea and sees what I've

done to Gina. She's so startled that she drops the tray—and growls.

We rush to stop Fifi from repoodling Gina's hair, and there's no more talk about the Academy.

By the time we get Gina out of the house, it's 4:45. Gina is a gorgeous bride—perfect hair, perfect dress, perfect makeup. Fifi walks at her side, holding the hem of the wedding dress above the dandelions.

As we walk to the car, Gina says, "I do!"

"What, Mom?" Sunny says.

"I do! I do!"

"Are you all right, Gina?" I ask.

She nods enthusiastically. "I do! I do!"

Katarina flies up and raps on Gina's forehead with her little fist. "Knock, knock! Anybody home?"

"I do!"

Katarina sits on top of Gina's head and gives me a scornful look. "*This* is what love spells do. Till she gets married, her brain is Swiss cheese."

But I still know I did the right thing. Really. I know it. Really!

We reach Gina's faded red Hyundai, and Gina climbs in back. I say, "Gina? You have to drive."

"I do!" she says—but she doesn't budge.

Katarina says, "You can't expect a bride to chauffeur herself to her own wedding! It's just not done."

"But Gina's the only one who knows how to drive!"

"So, magic up a carriage. Don't be lazy! Find a pumpkin."

"We don't have time. Plus, the cops would pull a carriage over, for sure."

Fifi raises her hands like a dog raising its paws and begs, "Let me drive! I am a chauffeur *extraordinaire!*"

Sunny tells her, "But you need a license."

Fifi points at the dog tag hanging from her rhinestone collar. "I have ze license."

Sunny shakes her head. "That's the wrong kind of license."

"I am ze driver *excellent*! I am in ze car all ze time!"

I think about all the old fairy tales where the dog got turned into a coachman. It never seemed to be a problem then. (But when you think about it, a cat wearing boots wasn't a problem then, either.)

So I hand Fifi the keys and hope for the best.

ZOOOOOOM! We race toward the school, Fifi behind the wheel. And she is an excellent driver. Of course, she sticks her head out the window as she steers, but otherwise she does a great job.

"I do! I do!" Gina says from the backseat.

Sunny ignores her and asks me, "You're sure she'll go back to normal after the wedding?"

"Yes. The moment the moon is full, she'll be fine, and she'll be married, so she'll have gotten her dream."

Gina nods eagerly. "I do!"

Just as we turn in to the school parking lot, Fifi pulls the car to a screeching stop. Katarina splats against the inside of the windshield and then sits down on the dashboard, swearing. (If I ever become a truck driver, I've got all the vocabulary I'll ever need.)

"Fifi! What's wrong?" I ask.

Fifi leaps out of the car—which she's parked sideways over three spaces—and runs across the lawn. That's not easy in spike heels. She reaches a tree, stares up into it, and starts barking.

Has she gone crazy?

No. She's seen a squirrel. It sits on a high branch, chattering, as Fifi runs all around the tree, panting and barking. (The squirrel's name is Seymour, and I could tell you a lot about him, but that's a different story.)

"Do you think Fifi will be okay?" Sunny asks.

"She's not going to budge from that tree. We'll take her home after the wedding."

We all get out of the car and head for the door.

CHAPTER

30

Paige is waiting for us when we walk into the cafeteria. Not cafeteria—wedding chapel. (Does that make it a chapelteria?)

With all the flowers and flickering candles, it's truly gorgeous in here. It even smells good—like roses, orange blossoms, and chocolate cake.

Paige looks at Gina and says, "*Ooooooh!* I knew that was the best dress!" It takes her a minute or two to admire every detail, and then we lead Gina to the back of the room.

I ask Paige, "Is Coach Overdale here with the minister?"

"Not yet."

I check the time on my cell phone. It's a minute to five.

I duck out into the hallway to see if the coach is anywhere in sight. There's no sign of him, but I do see Scott heading in to the gym, and he sees me.

"Lacey, what are you doing here already? The game doesn't start for two hours."

"Why are *you* here?"

"I wanted to go over Coach's playbook. He always says you can never be too prepared."

"Are you really disappointed you're not in the game?"

"I was at first. *Really* disappointed. But you know . . . I had a great time coaching the team this morning. I'm a way better coach than player. I want you in the gym at 6:45 sharp!"

Wow, he even sounds like a coach. I tell him, "No problem! See you then!" He gives me a thumbs-up and goes in to the gym.

I look down the hall for Coach Overdale, hoping to see him walking in the front door with the minister. Where are they?

By 5:30 we're all getting really worried. Paige looks at the clock and says, "I can't miss the basketball game. I'm cheering, and my dad's coming to watch!" I think about how I'm supposed to play in the game, but push the thought away. There's just too much other stuff to think of—like, *Where is the coach?*

Sunny twists her hair in knots, the way she does when she gets nervous. "What if the love spell wore off and the coach isn't coming?"

Katarina, who looks crankier than she's been all week, says,

"If Gina doesn't get her dream, she'll be unhappy for the rest of her life. But who needs happiness?"

Sunny says, "My mom does!"

And everybody looks at me. All I can say is, "I'm sure the coach will be here any second!"

Katarina says, "*I'm* sure you're leading them into ruination. Not one love spell, but two! Two!"

The only person in the room who doesn't seem to be worried is Gina, who's stopped saying, "I do," and is now picking apart a daisy and murmuring, "He loves me . . . he loves me . . . he loves me . . ."

Katarina shouts, "And *I* love you not! ZIP IT!"

Gina looks confused. "Zip what?"

Katarina pounds her head against the wall and mutters, "It *had* to be a love spell!"

Then, finally, the doors open, and Coach Overdale strides in. Hooray! He sees Gina across the room and shouts, "Sunny's mother! I LOVE YOU THIS MUCH!" He spreads his arms as wide as he can.

"I do! I do! I do!" Gina shouts. She hurls herself across the room, more like a linebacker than a bride—and almost knocks him down as she leaps into his arms.

"Sunny's mother!"

"I do!"

"Sunny's mother!"

"I do!"

Katarina can't take it anymore and pulls out her wand. "Don't make me use this!"

I say, "Katarina, calm down!" And then I walk up to Gina and the coach. "Coach, let go of her! Gina, you can't say, 'I do,' until the end of the ceremony."

The coach looks heartbroken as he puts Gina down. He sticks out his lower lip like a five-year-old and says, "But I want to marry Sunny's mother!"

"So, where's the minister?"

"He's christening a baby. But he said he'll be here the second he's done."

"When will that be?"

"Seven thirty at the latest."

Seven thirty? That would mean I can't play in the game. "I told you the wedding was at five!"

"I tried everybody in town. But I love Sunny's mother so much that I don't mind waiting!"

Gina leaps into his arms again. "I do! I do! I do!"

Katarina raises her wand and says, "That's it! You're toast! At least toast is quiet!"

Sunny jumps in front of her mother. "Stop it! She can't help it!"

I shout, "EVERYBODY, CALM DOWN!"

They all look at me like I know what I'm doing. How am I supposed to choose between the wedding and the basketball game? The wedding is really, really important—and Gina will be miserable for the rest of her life if the ceremony doesn't happen (not to mention that everyone in the world will hate me)—but I promised Scott and Dad that I would play in the game. It was one thing when the wedding was at five and the game was at seven. That might have worked, but I can't do both at the same time!

Or can I?

I take a deep breath and think, maybe I *can* do them both. I want to be there at the start of the wedding, just to make sure everything works. But after that, the ceremony can go on without me. I can play in the game and run back and check on things whenever there's a break.

It'll be a piece of cake—a piece of *wedding* cake.

I need to separate Gina and the coach before Katarina turns one of them into toast. So I lead Gina out of sight behind a huge arrangement of orchids, telling her, "It's bad luck for him to see you before the ceremony. You know that, right?"

She nods.

Then I go back to the coach and pull him into the room's farthest corner. "You stay here and be quiet. Can you do that?"

He nods, too.

So now, all we have to do is wait.

And wait.

And wait.

CHAPTER
31

At 6:45 p.m., Paige and I leave the others behind and hurry into the gym. The bleachers are almost full, and everybody's wearing the purple and gold school colors. Most people wear sweatshirts, but Mr. Griffith is extra flashy in a purple scarf and a gold vest.

Mrs. Brinker grabs Paige's arm and shouts, "Your cheer squad is in a shambles in the locker room. Go in there, get dressed, and take control!"

"Yes, Mrs. Brinker."

As Paige scurries away, she sees her dad already sitting in the bleachers. I know how hard it is for Dr. Harrington to take time off from the hospital, so it's a really big deal that he's here. He's got a cell phone in one hand and a camera in the other— and when Paige waves at him, he takes a picture of her with each. (If Gina weren't under a love spell, she'd be doing the same thing.)

Then it's *my* turn to get yelled at. Scott sees me and shouts, "Lacey! Change your clothes and start warming up! Remember, we're counting on you!"

Oh no! My uniform!

Suddenly, I hear loud whistling, clapping, and shouting from the end of the bleachers. Dad, Mom, and Madison are sitting in the front row, cheering me on. At first, I think they're waving banners, but then I realize they're holding pieces of my uniform. Dad has the shirt, Mom has the shorts, and Madison has the socks. I sigh with relief and grab my clothes.

"Good luck!" Dad says.

"Thanks! I'll need it!"

Will I ever.

I hold the wand in my hand as I wait in the girls' locker room for the game to begin. I've come up with a spell that will give me a little tiny bit of basketball magic: "This isn't a drill, I need some skill!"

All I have to do is chant the spell and toss it at myself. A little magic is all I need to be a winner.

Actually, a little magic is all I need to be a *cheater*.

Magic is easy.

With magic, I could win anything I want, but it wouldn't mean anything, would it? I'm pretty sure I'd just end up feeling rotten afterward.

And without magic, that leaves plain old me: a cruddy player right in the middle of things in the first game of the season. It's really scary! I'm going to disappoint everybody!

Then I make a really, really hard decision: it's better to be sucky than to be a cheat.

Scott knocks on the locker room door and shouts, "Come on, Lacey! The game's starting!"

I stick the wand into the pocket of my basketball shorts and head out.

The game begins. Because our new mascot hasn't been chosen yet, tonight it's the Harry S. Truman Wolverines versus the Lincoln Nothings.

Since I'm both magic-free and talent-free, my big plan for the game is to never, ever get the ball.

And for a while, my plan works. I run away from the ball like it's going to bite me.

I get guarded by this really big kid who looks like he should be in college, not middle school. (I take that back. He looks like he should be in jail.) He's about nine feet tall—ten feet once you add his blond Mohawk—and has beady little eyes that look

straight through me. Even if I wanted to get the ball, Mohawk Boy would make that impossible.

Uh, *almost* impossible. Because right before the end of the first quarter, Dylan Hernandez throws the ball at me and I catch it. (So there goes my never-get-the-ball plan, right out the window.) I dribble the ball down the court, and Mohawk Boy slams into me. Ooooff! I stagger, but—just barely—manage not to fall down.

The ref blows his whistle and calls an intentional foul. I try to tell him I'm fine and that we should keep playing the game, but it's hard to talk when all the air has been knocked out of your lungs.

The ref doesn't make me shoot a free throw—he makes me shoot two. And I miss them both. (I'm pretty impressed when one of them actually hits the backboard.) The crowd groans. Wow. I've never disappointed a hundred people at once before.

The buzzer sounds, and Scott rushes up to me. "Lacey? Are you all right?"

"Yeah, I'm fine. I'm really sorry."

"That big jerk should have gotten kicked out of the game. Let's talk about how you can work around him."

I don't have time to discuss how to work around Mohawk Boy—I need to go check on the wedding. But Scott pulls me into a huddle with the rest of the team, and the two-minute break between quarters is over before I know it. I sure hope that the minister has shown up.

The game's second quarter doesn't go any better for me than the first, but because of Scott's coaching, the score is surprisingly close. Toward the end of the quarter we're actually up by a point. Then, for the third time tonight, I get the ball and try to make a basket—and hit Mohawk Boy right on the head.

He clutches his face and stumbles around the court like I'd hit him with a sledgehammer. Then he collapses to the ground with a loud thud.

I can't believe I hurt him! I've hit loads of people on the head with basketballs, and this never happened before.

Dr. Harrington sprints off the bleachers and kneels next to Mohawk Boy—who gives me a mean little smirk. That *faker!*

Dr. Harrington says, very loudly, "I'm worried about you, son. I think we'll have to shave your head and do a brain scan."

Mohawk Boy miraculously recovers and sits up. "I'm all right. Don't shave my head, dude!"

Dr. Harrington gives me a wink and goes back to his seat. So I wasn't the only one who knew Mohawk Boy was faking.

But the ref's not doing any winking. He calls another intentional foul, and because of me, the Wolverines get two free throws. Mohawk Boy makes them both, which puts us a point behind.

The buzzer sounds for the fifteen-minute halftime. I can

hardly look at my teammates as the cheerleaders take the floor, with Paige in the lead. "Don't be finkin'—root for Lincoln!" Paige cheers. I'm finkin', in more ways than one.

From across the gym, Scott tries to flag me down as the rest of the team gathers around him. I pretend not to see and run as fast as I can toward the cafeteria.

If you're ever in charge of a wedding, don't schedule a basketball game at the same time.

I hurry into the cafeteria shouting, "Is he here? Is he here?"

And then I see him: a minister in a black suit and a white collar, standing next to Sunny. Thank goodness!

I run up to him and give him a big hug. (You're probably not supposed to do that, but I can't help myself.) "Thank you so much for doing this!"

The minister clears his throat and looks uncomfortable. "I'm happy to perform the ceremony, but I'm on a very tight schedule. Friday is bingo night, and I have to be back by eight."

"No problem! Let's get going."

Sunny says, "Little tiny problem."

"What is it?"

"We can't find my mom."

"What do you mean, you can't find your mom?"

"She was behind the big flower arrangement. But when I

went to get her just now, she wasn't there, and the side door was open."

I can't help myself. I SCREAM.

The minister jumps and looks at me like I've gone bonkers, which I pretty much have. He checks his watch and starts backing away.

"No, wait!" I say.

Coach Overdale wanders over and says dreamily, "Can I do 'I do' now? Because I do. I really do do."

The minister stares at the coach, then hurries toward the door. "I'm sorry, but this all seems rather irregular. And I have bingo."

"Please, don't leave! Please! I'll find Gina. She's probably just in the bathroom or something."

"Call me next week. Perhaps we can reschedule."

Next week's too late! What am I going to do? I pull out my wand and chant the first spell I can think of: "No more bingo till Gina wears a ring-o." And then I zap him.

The minister stops in his tracks and turns around with a smile. He says, "Who cares about bingo? Gina needs a ring-o." He walks under the orange-blossom arch to wait.

Katarina's been hiding from the minister, but now she flies down and lands on his head. She snaps at me, "This is just great! Now *everybody's* under a spell. Girls, go find the bride, and let's finish this fiasco."

The coach says, "I'll help!" He starts calling, "Sunny's mother! Where are you!"

Katarina flies over and flutters in front of his face. "Buster, sit down and shut up." Her face really does look mean.

The coach sits down without another word.

CHAPTER

32

Sunny and I run out the side door and search up and down the halls of the school, looking for Gina.

"Mom! Mom!" Sunny calls.

"Gina! It's time for the wedding!" I yell.

But we can't find her anywhere.

When we walk by the gym, we hear Mr. Griffith talking to the crowd. "Ladies and gentlemen, it's time for you to vote on the two finalists in the mascot competition."

"What's he talking about?" I say. Then I remember— halftime is when we're supposed to be doing our Bridemonsters runoff. Only, we're not doing it. So what *is* Mr. Griffith talking about?

We poke our heads inside the gym—and Sunny clutches my arm, horrified. "OMG! It's Mom!"

Sure enough, Gina stands in the middle of the floor next to

Mr. Griffith, and the kid in the grizzly-bear suit towers over both of them. Mr. Griffith says, "It's time to choose! Should we be the Lincoln Grizzlies—"

The grizzly kid ROARS and claws the air. The audience applauds.

"—or should we be the Lincoln Bridemonsters?"

Gina looks confused and says quietly, "I do?" (Now it's the audience's turn to look confused.)

Paige, who's been standing with the cheerleaders, runs over to us. "There you are! I didn't know how to stop it!"

"What happened?" I ask.

"Gina walked in during halftime, and Mr. Griffith saw the dress. He asked her if she was supposed to be the Bridemonster, and she said, 'I do! I do!' He said she was just in time for the mascot runoff."

On the gym floor, Mr. Griffith looks at Gina and the Grizzly and says, "Okay, mascots. Knock our socks off."

Gina just stands there sweetly, but the Grizzly runs up to the bleachers roaring and shouting, "Go, Lincoln!"

Sunny calls, "Mom—the minister's here. It's time to get married! Come on!"

Gina smiles and trots toward us.

But her path is blocked by the Grizzly. *ROAR!*

She tries to go around him on one side. *ROAR!*

She tries to go around him on the other. *ROAR!*

She tries to be polite. "Excuse me, but I have a wedding to go to."

And he *ROARS* louder than ever, and raises his paws to block her way.

Gina loses it. She turns red and shrieks, "Get out of my way, bear! This is my special day! AND YOU'RE RUINING IT!"

The Grizzly doesn't back down. He ROARS again.

Gina attacks. *WHAM!* She tackles the Grizzly and knocks him to the ground. She punches him with both fists (good thing it's a padded costume). And while she's punching him, she shouts, "I've been waiting and waiting! I have the dress! I have

the fiancé! I have the minister! And nothing, not even you"—punch-punch-punch—"will stop me from getting married!"

The Grizzly whimpers and tries to crawl away, but now Gina jumps on his back and starts biting his ear. (Good thing to know: if you get between an enchanted bride and her wedding, she turns into a Bridemonster.)

Martin Shembly sees us from the bleachers and shouts at Sunny, "Your mom is *AWESOME*!"

The stunned crowd seems to agree with him. Everyone starts applauding, cheering, whistling, and stomping.

Sunny, Paige, and I run out onto the gym floor. It takes all three of us to pull Gina off the terrified Grizzly. As we lead her out, the room thunders with a chant of "BRIDEMONSTER! BRIDEMONSTER! BRIDEMONSTER!"

Paige has to stay behind in the gym to cheer, so Sunny and I bring Gina back into the cafeteria. Katarina sits on the coach's shoulder, still guarding him.

Katarina sees Gina's red face and smeary makeup and asks, "What happened to *her*?"

"She got in a fight with a grizzly bear," I say.

Katarina doesn't even blink. "Grizzlies can be worse than trolls."

The coach looks at Katarina and asks, "Little fairy lady, may I leave the chair now?"

"Yes."

The coach jumps up, runs over, takes Gina in his arms, and whirls her around and around. He says, "Oh, darling! Never leave me again."

The minister watches, his head swaying with each whirl.

Katarina says, "Let's get moving! We've got a bride! We've got a groom! We've got a minister!"

I say, "Wait a second! Shouldn't we fix Gina's makeup?"

Katarina shakes her head. "The coach wouldn't notice if she was covered in slime."

That's kind of sad—but completely true.

I say, "Before we get started, I do want to do one thing. The maid of honor needs a dress."

I zap Sunny's clothes, which swirl around her and are transformed into a gown made of rich green velvet with a sparkling trim of real diamonds. They'll disappear at midnight but they'll sure look pretty till then. "Oooh!" Sunny says.

"*Now* we're ready!"

Sunny gives me a hug. "Thank you, Lacey."

The coach is *still* whirling Gina around, and they're both looking queasy. "It's time," I say.

He puts Gina down and nods, glassy-eyed. "Must . . . marry . . . Sunny's . . . mother."

I give him a little push. "Go wait next to the minister."

The coach weaves over to the orange-blossom arch.

I look at Katarina, hoping she'll be impressed, but all she does is pull out her notebook and start writing notes. I don't care if she doesn't approve of the love spells. It was the only way to get this done.

"Will you walk your mother down the aisle?" I ask Sunny, who nods. As she slowly leads her mother toward the coach and the minister, I stand in the back of the room, breathing a sigh of relief. I got Gina her dream! I did it!

But . . .

Gina and the coach seem hypnotized. Even the minister seems hypnotized. Nobody's eyes are really focused. To be honest, it's a tiny bit creepy.

I watch Gina walking toward the coach, smiling a quiet smile. A little voice in my head reminds me that Gina has never been a quiet-smile kind of person. She's more of a belly-laugh kind of person. But this is a wedding. It's not a belly-laugh event.

Darn it, I'm doing the right thing! I'm sure of it: 100 percent sure.

Almost completely 100 percent sure.

The coach takes Gina's hand, and the minister smiles and says, "Dearly beloved . . ."

. . . and I hear the faint sound of a buzzer.

OMG! The basketball game!

CHAPTER 33

I run back to the gym just as the last quarter starts. The score on the scoreboard is Truman Wolverines 36, Lincoln Nothings 35.

"Lacey! Where were you? You missed the whole third quarter!" Scott cries.

"Sorry . . . I got trapped in the cafeteria." Which is true.

"GO, LACEY!" Mom, Dad, and Madison shout from the bleachers. I wave and play as hard as I can. I don't want to be the reason we lose this game. If I can just keep out of everybody's way, we can still win.

But as the game winds down, it gets harder and harder to keep away from Mohawk Boy. Every time the ref turns his head, the big creep elbows me or gives me a push.

With five seconds left in the game, we're still one point down.

And I've got the ball.

Oh, puke. I'm going to make us lose the game for sure. But I have to at least try . . .

I raise the ball to shoot—

WHAM! Mohawk Boy rams into me like a freight train—and this time he knocks me right off my feet.

I glide over the waxed floor like a hockey puck and slide under a stack of gymnastic equipment in the corner of the gym.

I lie there a second, the wind knocked out of me. As I try to catch my breath, I'm surprised to hear the sound of sobbing. I peer over and see Principal Nazarino leaning on the parallel bars as Mrs. Brinker pats her shoulder. "Gina, you're better off without him," Mrs. Brinker tells her.

Gina?

Principal Nazarino sobs, "I thought Brian loved me!"

What are they talking about?

You've probably figured it out already, but remember, *I* just got knocked halfway across the gym by Mohawk Boy. The wheels are turning in my head—but not very well. It's more like they're grinding and wobbling. I keep repeating to myself, *"Gina?"*

Scott pulls me out from under a pommel horse and back onto my feet. "Lacey, are you okay?"

"Gina?" I say out loud.

Scott decides that this means yes and pushes me toward the court. "The ref gave you two free throws because of the foul.

There's no time left on the clock—but you can still win the game for us!"

The wobbly wheels in my head grind to a stop, and then start turning back to the game. Free throws? I can't make free throws!

As Scott walks me toward the center of the court, he says, "I've been watching you tonight, and your problem is in your follow-through. You can be a good player! Coach Overdale always says it's all in the wrist!"

He walks away, and the ref hands me the ball. Two hundred eyes are on me as I look at the basket.

What a stupid piece of advice. Scott sounds a little like Katarina when she first taught me how to use the wand: *Picture where you want the spell to go, and then toss it.*

Wait a minute. Could basketball be that simple? Is throwing a basketball like tossing a spell?

I guess I'm going to find out, because I look right at the basket and picture the ball going into it. Then I throw.

SWISH!

It goes right in.

The crowd cheers, and Paige and the cheerleaders shake their pom-poms and chant, "Lacey Unger-Ware! She's our man! If she can't do it, no one can!" And out of the corner of my eye, I can see Dad jumping up and down like his feet are on fire.

The ref tosses me the ball for my second free throw. I take

a few deep breaths to focus on the basket, and suddenly, for the first time since Mohawk Boy knocked me down, I see things clearly. I see *everything* clearly.

OMG! OMG! OMG!

OMG!!!!!!

I screwed up, and I screwed up big-time!

I've been fairy-godmothering the wrong Gina!

Let me say that one more time:

I'VE BEEN FAIRY-GODMOTHERING THE WRONG GINA!

It wasn't Gina, Sunny's mother, who was supposed to get her dream wedding with her true love.

It was Gina Nazarino, Lincoln Middle School principal!

I didn't even know she *had* a first name!

I'm so upset that I fling the basketball away without even thinking about it, and the ball swishes into the basket for the second time. The crowd goes wild—the game is over, and we've won.

But I barely notice, because all I keep thinking is that I've got to stop the wedding!

The clues come together in my head:

How Principal Nazarino was so interested in girlie-girl wedding dresses. How she got so mad this morning when she heard the coach was going to marry somebody else. How, at the

Bat-n-Putt, the coach talked about love being in the air. And how he just happened to have an engagement ring ready to go.

They must have been dating all along and not wanted people at school to know.

I am so stupid. Last night the coach didn't go to *Sunny's* house to propose—he went to *Gina Nazarino's* house to propose. I was wrong about everything.

As I race toward the gym door, all the boys on the team surround me, cheering.

Scott gives me a big hug. "You did it."

When I manage to squirm away from the boys, more cheering people block my path. It's like every single person in the gym wants to high-five me or slap me on the back.

Paige makes her way through the crowd, grinning from ear to ear. "Way to go, Lacey!"

But I just tell her, "I've got to stop the wedding—it's the wrong Gina!"

Because the wheels in Paige's head turn really, really well, she instantly gets what's going on: "But you saw the coach with an engagement ring!"

"It wasn't for Sunny's mom, Gina—it was for Principal *Gina* Nazarino."

"But you asked the love locator."

"I asked the wand if the coach was *Gina's* true love. I didn't use last names."

Paige turns pale. "Oh, Lacey!"

Just then, I see an opening in the crowd. "Come on, let's go!"

Paige and I squeeze between, under, and around people. Every second counts when you've got a wedding to stop—and I've lost a lot of seconds!

We finally make it to the door. I hope we're not too late.

CHAPTER 34

Paige and I run down the empty hallway shouting, "STOP THE WEDDING!"

We reach the cafeteria door and fling it open. We both shout at once: *"Stop the wedding!"*

Katarina and Sunny turn, stunned, but Gina (Sunny's mother, Gina—this is getting confusing!), the coach, and the minister don't even look at me—the spells I put on them are too strong.

The minister keeps droning on—and he's reached the part near the end where he says, "If any of you can show just cause why Coach Overdale and Sunny's mother may not lawfully be married, speak now; or else forever hold your peace."

I shout at the top of my lungs, "I OBJECT! THIS IS THE WRONG GINA! THE COACH IS SUPPOSED TO MARRY PRINCIPAL NAZARINO!"

The minister *still* doesn't pay any attention to me. "All right.

Since there are no objections, we may proceed with the vows."

Sunny runs up and tries to yank Gina away, but Gina stands as still as a stone. Because of the love spell, she wants to get married, and she's not going to budge till she does. "Mom, don't do this!" Sunny begs her, but Gina doesn't even seem to hear.

Paige waves her hands in front of the coach's face and yells, "Coach! Snap out of it!" She might as well be invisible.

The minister asks, "Do you, Coach Overdale, take Sunny's mother to be—"

I shout, "We've got to stop this before he says, 'I do!'"

Katarina flies over and dive-bombs the minister's head, but he just swats her away like a pesky bug.

The minister continues: ". . . your lawfully wedded wife, to have and to hold . . ."

What am I going to do?

". . . as long as you both shall live?"

Coach Overdale takes a deep breath and says, "I— OOOOOFFFFFF!!!!"

The *ooofff* is because I just hit him on the head with a plastic garbage can. Garbage spills all over the floor.

The can doesn't knock the coach down the way I hoped it would. He just bobbles a little and turns back to the minister and says, "I—"

Then I see a Tic Tac box on the floor. A *familiar* Tic Tac box. I grab it.

"WAIT!" I yell, waving the box in front of the coach's face. I tell him, "You're about to kiss the bride. It's the most important kiss of your entire life. Don't you want your breath to be minty fresh?"

The coach blinks at me, thinking.

Sunny and Paige look at me like I've gone crazy, and I motion to them to hold their noses.

Just like I hoped he would, the coach puts a hand up to his mouth, sniffs his own breath, and frowns. He takes the Tic Tac box away from me and pops it open right in front of his face.

There's a whoosh of air, and he gets blasted by the smell of an entire cafeteria's worth of tuna-roni and feet.

The coach stumbles backward, trips over the garbage can, and *wham*! He hits his head against the wall and falls to the ground.

As the tuna-roni/feet smell floats over the room like a dark cloud, Gina and the minister start coughing. The stink was bad before, but now that it's been cooped up in a little plastic box, it's a hundred times worse.

The minister covers his face with his hands and lurches out the back door.

Gina looks like she's about to throw up (the smell is that bad), so Sunny leads her outside, too.

Paige and I kneel down to look at the coach. "He's out cold," Paige says.

I pat his cheeks. "Wake up! Wake up!"

Katarina fans him with her wings, but his eyelids don't even flicker.

So Paige and I grab his feet and drag him out of the smelly room. He weighs a ton, and his head keeps clunking on the floor, but we finally get him outside onto the lawn.

Nearby, Sunny sits on a bench with Gina, who's got her head between her knees as she tries not to puke. "Is the coach all right?" Sunny asks.

I shake the coach's shoulders. "Come on! Wake up!" He just lies there, not moving.

The minister walks up and asks him: "Do you take Sunny's mother to be your lawfully wedded wife?"

Paige says, "He can't hear you."

"Oh, how silly of me." So the minister leans down and shouts as loud as he can: "DO YOU TAKE SUNNY'S MOTHER TO BE YOUR LAWFULLY WEDDED WIFE?"

Katarina, floating nearby, grumbles, "I'm surrounded by idiots."

I tell Paige, "Take the minister over to the bench and try to make him be quiet."

She nods at me and leads the minister away, telling him, "We can't finish the ceremony right now."

"Why?"

"Because the coach isn't feeling well."

"Why?"

"He just isn't."

"Why?"

This could go on all night.

I pat the coach's cheeks again. He still doesn't wake up. "The coach needs a doctor—where's your dad?" I ask Paige.

"He's probably already in the car, waiting for me. I'll get him." She starts to get up, but the minister grabs her hand and says, "Why?"

"*I'll* get your dad," I say.

As I run to the parking lot, I pass Principal Nazarino. She's leaning against her car, and her eyes are red from crying. "Lacey, what's happening?"

I stop long enough to tell her, "I've got to get Dr. Harrington. There's something wrong with the coach!"

Principal Nazarino claps her hands over her mouth, shocked. "Where is he?" she asks.

I point back to the cafeteria and start running again.

When I reach Dr. Harrington's car, he's inside checking his e-mails. Thank goodness! I pound on the window and shout, "Come quick! We need your help!"

It only takes a minute for Dr. Harrington and me to get back to the lawn in front of the cafeteria.

We find Principal Nazarino sitting on the ground holding the coach's hand. "Brian, wake up! I know I was mad at you, but I love you."

Dr. Harrington kneels and checks the coach's pulse. Then he gently pushes back one of the coach's eyelids with his thumb and gets a worried look on his face. I couldn't have truly hurt him, could I? I look over and see Katarina perched on a tree branch, also looking worried. Oh, geez.

Paige's dad stands up and says, "I'll be right back. I've got an emergency kit in my car."

Katarina opens up her notebook and starts writing. She mutters, "This is really not going to look good in my report to the Godmother Academy."

She is *so* helpful.

CHAPTER

35

While we wait for Dr. Harrington to come back with the emergency kit, Principal Nazarino sits by the coach, her eyes full of tears. "Brian, wake up! Wake up!" But he doesn't seem to hear.

This is horrible!

Principal Nazarino whispers, "Brian, *please* wake up! I love you!" She leans down and kisses him on the lips.

And a moment later—a *wonderful* moment later—the coach's eyes open, and he smiles.

A pink light shines down on them, and streamers and confetti fall from the sky. The coach sits up, and he and Principal Nazarino hug like they never want to let each other go.

"What's happening?" I ask Katarina.

Katarina clasps her hands and sighs. "It's something very

rare! It's true love's kiss! Principal Razapino broke your idiotic spell with her love."

"You mean Nazarino?"

"Whatever."

On the bench, Gina—Sunny's mother Gina—looks at Sunny, bewildered. "Have I been sleepwalking? I've been having the strangest dream!" The kiss must have broken the spell on her, too. (But not on the minister, who's still smiling goofily. He'll be stuck that way till midnight.)

Sunny studies her mother's face and smiles. "Mom! You're back!" Gina flings her arms around Sunny and gives her a big, happy hug.

Sunny's mom doesn't notice—but I do—when the engagement ring that the coach gave her slips off her finger.

Plink, plink, roll! The ring bounces its way right to the coach's feet. He picks it up and looks at it, surprised.

Principal Nazarino asks him, "What's that?"

"It's my grandmother's engagement ring."

The coach helps Principal Nazarino to her feet, then goes down on one knee. "Gina Nazarino, will you marry me?"

"Yes! Yes! Yes!"

He slips the ring on her finger, and they kiss. I thought the other proposal was the most romantic thing I'd ever seen, but that was just love-spell playacting compared to this. This kiss is *epic*.

The coach tells Principal Nazarino, "I don't want to wait! Let's fly to Las Vegas tonight and get married!"

A little of the light goes out of her eyes. *Oh no.* Las Vegas may have Elvis, but I'm pretty sure it won't have Principal Nazarino's dream wedding.

I look at the clock on the school sign—it's 8:32. That gives us fifty-one minutes before the official time of the full moon, at 9:23. I can still give Principal Nazarino her dream wedding. We've got the groom, and we've got the minister.

But then I stop myself. Part of the reason I wanted to make the wedding work is that it was Sunny's mother's dream. I would be doing it for her, and I would also be doing it for Sunny. And it made being sent away to the Academy seem almost worth it.

But I don't even know Principal Nazarino—not really. She's just a woman who yells at me when I run in the hall at school. Do I really care if she gets her dream wedding?

If I don't complete my fairy-godmother assignment, everyone on earth will hate me. But I won't have to go away to the Academy, and I can stay in my room and never go out. It won't be very nice, but at least I'll still be with my family. And maybe, somehow, I'll be able to fix the hating part later on.

It's not my fault the fairies gave Principal Nazarino a fairy-godmother-in-training who's not very good: *me*. And it's not my fault she'll be miserable for the rest of her life because she doesn't get her dream wedding.

Oh, wait. It *is* my fault.

I look at Principal Nazarino's face as she tells the coach, "I think Las Vegas would be okay." But she doesn't look happy about it.

She's not just a principal who yells at me, she's a person whose life I'm about to ruin. So, when Principal Nazarino puts on a brave smile and says, "Brian, let's go to Vegas. Who needs a wedding dress?" I have to jump in.

"*You* do," I say.

Katarina goes, *"Phew!"* like she's been holding her breath the whole time I've been deciding.

I grab the principal's hand. "I really, really need to talk to you."

"Can't it wait?"

"No! Please, this will only take a second! It's an emergency!"

Principal Nazarino has been hearing kids talk to her about their emergencies for years—and what makes her a good principal is that she listens to them. She tells the coach, "I'll be right back."

And I lead her away.

CHAPTER

36

Principal Nazarino and I stand behind a school bus, where no one can see us, while Katarina flutters in the shadows.

The principal asks me, "All right, Lacey. What's this about?"

I curtsy and give the standard fairy-godmother speech: "Greetings and salutations! I am your fairy godmother! Not every girl receives this boon, but you are one of the lucky few!"

Katarina, hovering behind the principal's head, gives me a thumbs-up.

Principal Nazarino raises an eyebrow.

"I *know* it sounds crazy—" I say.

"Yes, it does. But I'll be happy to meet with you about it on Monday."

Katarina frowns and gives me a thumbs-down.

I could stand here arguing with Principal Nazarino all night, but she still wouldn't believe me. So I pull my wand out of the pocket of my basketball shorts and chant, "Time for the dress, so we'll have success!"

The principal's plain white blouse, sweater, and gray skirt swirl with magic sparkles, and I stand back, waiting for the elegant Grecian wedding dress to appear. But this time, instead of just white sparkles, there are also bands of pink and red. The sparkles disappear with a flash of light, leaving behind a wedding dress.

Uh-oh. It's not the tasteful white wedding dress I expected. It's an over-the-top, princessy dress with a poufy net skirt, pink lace, and a lot of big embroidered red roses. It's the dress Madison picked out! This is *awful!*

Principal Nazarino pats the dress, her mouth hanging open. "How did you do this?"

"I told you: I'm your fairy godmother."

The principal looks around. "Is this for a TV show? Where's the camera?"

I take her hand. "No, Principal Nazarino. There's no camera. I'm telling you the truth. Your dream is for a perfect wedding with your true love, and my job is to give it to you. I'm sorry that the dress isn't quite right."

I point to her reflection in a school-bus window, and she stares. It's the first time she's seen how she looks in the dress.

"OMG!" she says, sounding exactly like one of us kids.

"Maybe I can change it," I say.

"Change it? It's what I've dreamed of my whole life!" She twirls around, looking at her reflection. And she's smiling!

She finally tells me, "I saw a wedding dress like this when I was five years old, and I told everybody, 'When I get married, *this* is the one I want.' And here it is. How did you know?"

I *didn't* know. There must be some fairy-godmother magic going on that I don't understand yet. I guess that's what the hundred years of school is for.

Principal Nazarino doesn't wait for an answer. She just hugs me and says, "Of course you know. You're my fairy godmother!" With her glowing, smiling face, somehow the dress isn't over the top anymore. It's as beautiful as something out of a fairy tale.

I ask her, "You *do* want to get married tonight?"

She frowns a little. "You mean in Las Vegas?"

"No! Here! Just to make sure . . . Your true love *is* Coach Overdale?"

She nods enthusiastically. At least I got that right.

I tell her, "Everything is ready. Wait till you see how beautiful the wedding chapel is."

Katarina coughs loudly and shakes her head.

Principal Nazarino whirls, sees the fluttering fairy, and gasps.

"That's my assistant," I say. "Katarina, is there something you wanted to tell me?"

Annoyed at her new job title, Katarina points a finger at the cafeteria. "Somebody set off a stink bomb in the wedding chapel, remember?"

Principal Nazarino looks outraged. "Who did that?"

Katarina points at me. "It was a certain fairy godmother I know."

Oh, geez. Katarina's right! There's no way the cafeteria is going to work. I'll never be able to find another place before the full moon!

Now I wish I'd stuck with my plan to have the wedding in the park. There wouldn't have been a smell problem there.

Wait a minute. Why *not* have it in the park? I tap my cheek, thinking. I'd need to go there first and magically decorate it for the wedding. Then Sunny and Paige could walk over with Coach Overdale and the minister—it's only two blocks away. But Principal Nazarino shouldn't have to walk—not on her wedding day, and not in high heels!

In a fancy wedding, doesn't the bride arrive in a limo? I look around the parking lot and see Sunny's mom's Hyundai, parked sideways, just the way we left it. I raise my wand and chant, "The bride needs a ride!"

The Hyundai stretches, and stretches, and stretches, with its paint turning from faded red to shiny black. I didn't know a limousine could have that many windows.

I walk to the car and open the back door with a flourish. "Principal Nazarino, your carriage awaits!"

As she gets in, Principal Nazarino says, "This car is bigger than my entire apartment!"

Katarina looks at the limo and shakes her head.

"What's wrong now?" I ask.

"She can wait in there all she wants. But without a driver, she's not going to get very far."

"We've got a driver," I say. I start whistling and calling: "Fifi! Fifi! Here, girl!"

A moment later, the bushes at the edge of the parking lot shake, and Fifi bursts out of them and runs up to us in her spike heels. "'Ave you zeen ze squirrel?"

"No, Fifi. I need you to drive a bride to a wedding."

Fifi's whole body shakes like she's wagging an invisible tail.

Two minutes later, I run into the school parking lot to find my family. The school's clock says it's 8:46. I need to get this show on the road.

Some of the people in the crowd have left after the basketball game, but there are still groups scattered around talking.

I see Mom, Dad, and Madison waiting by our car. Mom says, "There you are, Lacey! Where have you been?"

"I've been . . . helping plan a wedding."

Dad smiles. "Is it a mascot wedding? Is the Bridemonster marrying the Grizzly?"

"No! Principal Nazarino is marrying Coach Overdale in the park!"

I must be saying it a little louder than I meant to, because suddenly everybody in the parking lot turns to look at me.

Mrs. Brinker rushes over. "Lacey, are you serious?"

Mr. Griffith walks over, too. "What's this about somebody getting married?"

And before I know it, I'm surrounded by people. I was just going to get my family—but now that I think about it, it would be nice having a *lot* of people at the wedding.

So I climb up on the bumper of Dad's car and shout, loud

enough for the whole parking lot to hear, "Everybody! I have an announcement to make! I want to invite you all to the surprise wedding of Principal Nazarino and Coach Overdale!"

"Students, too?" Martin Shembly asks.

"Anybody who wants to come! Everybody, start walking to Fountain Park!"

But *I* don't walk to the park—I run.

CHAPTER 37

At 9:12 p.m., dozens of people have gathered in the park for the wedding of Principal Gina Nazarino and Coach Brian Overdale.

Mom, Dad, and Madison sit in the folding chairs I've magicked up near the fountain. Sunny and her mother sit right behind them.

Paige is the one who turned Gina's wedding dress into a cocktail dress. First, she trimmed two feet from the hem and pinned it up. Then she borrowed Mr. Griffith's purple scarf to make a belt—and Gina went from bride to guest in under three minutes.

Paige and Dr. Harrington are sitting with Sunny and her mom. In fact, Dr. Harrington and Gina are sitting next to each other. I thought they hated each other? Hmm . . . Maybe, after all these years, she's forgiven him for the prom.

I look around at the park. I know I'm bragging, but it's absolutely beautiful. Just like on the practice day, there are flowers and trees and lawn and water burbling in the fountain. I've also added hanging lanterns and—my favorite part—dozens of magical pink fireflies darting high overhead.

Coach Overdale waits next to the minister, his eyes gleaming in the lantern light. The limo pulls up to the edge of the park, and I run over to open the door. Katarina, who rode with the bride, darts out first and flies up toward the fireflies to blend in like she's one of them.

When Principal Nazarino gets out, I see that Fifi has redone her hair. To my relief, there's not a single poodle pouf in sight, just ringlets and tiny red rosebuds to match the dress. There are *ooohs* from the crowd when they see how beautiful she looks.

Principal Nazarino sees the park for the first time, and she *ooohs*, too. "It's perfect, Lacey! It's better than I ever dreamed."

Martin Shembly starts playing the "Wedding March" on his violin (he's a handy kid to have around!), and Principal Nazarino extends her hand to me. "Lacey, will you walk me down the aisle? This wouldn't be happening if it weren't for you."

"I'm still in my basketball uniform!"

"Which is perfect, since I'm marrying the coach."

Every eye is on Principal Nazarino as I escort her down the aisle. Madison whispers, loud enough for everyone to hear, "That lady picked *my* dress!"

When we reach him, the coach takes his bride's hand like he never wants to let go. I can tell that his love is not something that's going to wear off at midnight.

At 9:22, the minister says, "I now pronounce you husband and wife."

And everyone applauds as Principal Nazarino and Coach Overdale kiss. In the back, where nobody can see me, I wave my wand and make sweet-smelling rose petals fall from the sky over the bride, the groom, and all of us.

Oh, wow! I've done it! I've made Gina Nazarino's dream come true! I make a silent wish that she lives happily ever after.

That they both do.

CHAPTER

38

I t's just after midnight when Dad drives Mom, Madison, and me home. I was getting cold out in the park, so Dad gave me his jacket, and Katarina is back in a pocket one more time. Maybe for the last time.

I wonder if the fairies will take me away to the Godmother Academy tonight.

Everyone's chattering about the wedding party, which ended after a lot of laughing and dancing and eating magical cake. (I'm sure it disappeared from everyone's stomachs right at the stroke of midnight. It's the Lacey Unger-Ware diet plan.)

Mom and Dad know I helped with the ceremony, but they don't have a clue that I planned the whole thing. How could they? Even when Madison keeps saying she picked out the dress, our parents just think she's being her too-imaginative self.

"I was so surprised when you walked Principal Nazarino up

the aisle," Mom says. "I didn't think you knew her that well."

"We got friendly after I won the zoo internship," I say, feeling bad that one of the last things I say to Mom before I get sent away to the Academy is a total fib. I wish I could tell her and Dad the truth, but then I realize that I can tell them the part of the truth that matters the most. I swallow down a lump in my throat and say, "I love you guys."

If I say another word I'll cry.

Dad says, "I love you, Lacey."

Mom says, "*I* love you, Lacey."

And Madison says, "I love you, too!" and leans over and kisses me on the cheek.

There's the sound of a loud sob in the car. But it's not from me; it's from Katarina.

I go into my room and close the door. "Greetings and salutations, Lacey Unger-Ware!" a squeaky but surprisingly loud little voice says, and I jump about a foot.

A fairy flits up to me and smiles sweetly. She looks younger than Katarina, and her hair is an electric shade of blue that matches her electric-blue eyes exactly. Even the polish on her little fingernails is blue.

Katarina pokes her head out of my pocket and frowns. "Augustina Oberon! I heard you got demoted to dryer fairy."

Augustina's sweet smile vanishes. "And I heard you died.

Not true, I see. What a pity." My whole life is about to change, and they're busy insulting each other!

Augustina plasters her sweet smile back on and tells me, "You have passed your test triumphantly! Well done, my dear! Well done! Everyone at the Academy is so looking forward to meeting you! Are you ready to begin your education?"

"No! Please! I don't want to go!"

"Oh, piffle. You'll love it there! Besides, you don't have a choice." Augustina hovers near me and raises her wand. "The first day of a hundred years—"

"WAIT!" Katarina shouts.

Augustina pauses. "What is it?"

"Lacey never said good-bye to Julius."

Augustina purses her lips, but Katarina insists. "Let the poor girl say good-bye to dear little Julius. You've got to."

What's Katarina talking about? She doesn't even *like* Julius!

But Augustina lowers her wand. "Fine. Just make it speedy— we don't have all night."

Katarina flutters up to the ceiling and says, "Call him, Lacey."

Weird. Still, it would be nice to say good-bye. I go to the door and call, "Julius! Here, Julius!" And a moment or two later, Julius glides in, purring. Then he sees Augustina and—

CHOMP!

He leaps into the air and swallows her up in one quick gulp. *Aak!*

A muffled little voice comes from the direction of his stomach: "Get me out of here!"

I lean down by Julius and tell Augustina, "Don't worry. I know the Heimlich maneuver for cats. I'll get you right out."

Katarina zips back down and perches on my shoulder. "Don't you dare."

I look at her, confused.

Katarina cups her hands around her mouth and calls out, "Augustina! Do you hear me?"

"Yes, I hear you! Eww! There's cat food in here! It's disgusting! And there are hair balls! *EWW!* Get me out! GET ME OUT!"

"Of course we will. As soon as you agree." Katarina gives me a wink.

"Agree to what?" Augustina calls back.

Katarina paces on my shoulder like a lawyer making a big courtroom speech. "Lacey needs a hundred years of training, I admit. Possibly even two hundred. But it doesn't have to be at the Academy. I'm applying for permission to homeschool her right here."

Katarina could do that? That would be GREAT!

Augustina says, "Permission denied! Get me out of here."

My shoulders slump. It did sound too good to be true. I feel like crying.

But Katarina's not finished. "Augustina, do you hear that disgusting gurgling sound near your feet? That's Julius's small intestine. And it would like nothing better than to digest one blithering blue fairy."

There's a long, long pause. Julius plops down on the floor and starts to lick himself.

Augustina yells, "*EW!* More hair balls!" And there's a loud sneeze from inside Julius's stomach. "All right! All right! Permission granted! You can homeschool her. Just get me out!"

I'm so happy I could burst. "Thank you, Katarina! Thank you so much!"

Katarina flies up to my face and wags her finger at me. "It's not going to be easy, missy. With me here as your teacher, you're really going to have to work!"

"I will! I will!" I wish I could hug her, but I blow her a kiss instead.

Katarina catches the kiss. She looks embarrassed, but she doesn't open her hand to let the kiss back out.

Suddenly there's another loud gurgle from Julius's stomach and another scream from Augustina.

I ask Katarina, "Should I get her out?"

"What's your hurry?" Katarina looks fondly at Julius and says, "I love that cat!"

CHAPTER 39

It's six weeks later, and the gym is packed for the city championship. In the final seconds of the game, Dylan Hernandez passes me the ball.

Me, Lacey Unger-Ware.

And he passes me the ball because I'm good. Not magic good, but good good. With Scott's coaching and Dad's help, I really belong here.

I shoot—and the ball circles the rim.

OMG! It's not going in! I just lost the game!

And then, plunk! The ball goes through the net.

The buzzer sounds, and we win!

Paige and the cheerleaders set off their confetti cannon, and the room is filled with swirling paper.

Scott, who's been filling in while the coach is away on his honeymoon, picks me up and spins me around. "Lacey, you did great!"

"You're a great coach!"

Scott blushes and bats his beautiful eyelashes at me. Then, OOOOFFF! He tumbles to the gym floor, taking me with him. His terrible trio of little brothers have tackled him and made his knees buckle.

Scott looks over to make sure I'm okay—I am—and then says, "Excuse me a minute." He chases after the little boys, who run off giggling.

I get up, almost blinded by the falling confetti. I bump into Sunny, who's dressed in a Bridemonster mascot costume. After her mother beat up the Grizzly, the Lincoln Bridemonsters won in a landslide, so tonight, Sunny wears a thrift-store wedding dress, a veil, plastic fangs, and monster claws. "You look awesome!" I say. "New fangs?"

"Martin got them for me."

And then I see Martin Shembly standing next to her. He nods and says, "I got them online."

OMG. Martin's buying Sunny presents? Sure, it's just plastic fangs, but it's still really thoughtful. I can't wait to talk to Sunny about this later.

I walk away through the confetti storm . . .

. . . and run into Mom, Dad, and Madison. We have a family hug.

"Tell everyone there's a big victory party at the Hungry Moose tonight," Mom says. "Cake, ice cream, and purple and gold sprinkles!"

"Great shot at the end, honey!" Dad says to me.

Madison looks through the falling confetti toward the basketball net. "Well, the fairy helped, too, when she pushed it in."

Dad tousles Madison's hair. "You're so cute!"

"Daddy! Don't mess up my hair!"

Madison's got to be making that up, right? Just to be sure, I walk over to the basket and peer up at it. And there's Katarina sitting on the rim of the basket, swinging her legs like she's on a bench at the park.

"Katarina!" I hiss. "You get down here this instant!"

She flies down behind the bleachers, and I follow her.

"You're not supposed to help me win the game," I tell her.

"It was taking forever. And you've got homework."

"It's Friday night!"

"Fairy-godmother homework."

Geez. It's going to be such a pain having Katarina around as my full-time tutor—especially on Friday nights. I need to do something.

"Katarina, come with me to the party at the Hungry Moose. We're celebrating!"

"No parties!"

"There's going to be cake."

"No! Tonight we're studying techniques for identifying your client. You really stink at that."

"And ice cream."

"No!"

"And gallons and gallons and *gallons* of strawberry soda."

Katarina frowns at me. I think she's going to say "no" again, but instead she asks, "What time does this party start?"

Maybe having Katarina around won't be as bad as I thought. I'm sure going to find out.

ACKNOWLEDGMENTS

This book's many godparents include Emily Bergman, John Biondo, Teresa Blasberg, Helen Brauner, Tom Brauner, Becky Bristow, Josh Capps, Jennifer Cheng, Jennifer Collopy, Breezie Daniel, Dirk Dickens, Michelle Hardy, Lisa Holmes, Lauren Mattson, Maelena Mattson, Matt Mattson, Tom Mattson, Jen Mulder, Melonia Musser-Brauner, Dashiell Musser-Brauner, Jean Noble, Gerardo Paron, Daryl Patton, Michael Schenkman, Cheryl Tan, Linda Wachter, Daniel Wake, Alexis Wallrich, Justeen Ward, and Marty Ward. The support of the amazing Lucky 13s writing group has also been invaluable.

Thanks to Laura Hopper, Joseph Veltre, and Bayard Maybank, who have believed in this series, and in us, from the very beginning.

We especially want to thank our editor, Catherine Onder, who is truly a joy to work with. And thank you, thank you, *thank you* to everyone at Disney-Hyperion whose talent and hard work have gone into *The Magic Mistake*.

KEEP READING
FOR A
SNEAK PEEK
AT THE NEXT BOOK!

CHAPTER 1

For the first time ever, in like hundreds and hundreds of years, the Godmothers' League is letting a student be homeschooled instead of sent away to the Godmother Academy.

That student is me.

And where there's a student, there's got to be a teacher. *My* teacher is Katarina Sycorax, who's three inches tall with beautiful butterfly wings and a bad attitude. (By bad attitude, I mean she's cranky.)

I've had cranky teachers before, and I bet you have, too. But yours probably wasn't living on top of your dresser in your bedroom. And I'm sure yours didn't cut the arm off your favorite teddy bear to make herself a fur coat. Or threaten to turn you into an elephant if you didn't memorize your assignment. (Because everyone knows that elephants have excellent memories.)

For me, it's like the school day is twenty-four hours long and the bell never rings.

Katarina and I have been waiting for weeks to find out who my new fairy godmother client is, and we're both getting pretty antsy about it. When I get antsy, I chew my fingernails. When Katarina gets antsy, she yells. Like, all the time. Right now, she's yelling about my book report, which she's also stomping on.

"This stinks! Did you even bother to read *Godmothering During the Renaissance?*"

"Of course I did!"

The old, dusty book is still on my desk. Katarina flies over and tells it, "Book! Show me how far Lacey read!"

When the pages flip open and stop at Chapter Two, Katarina gives me an accusing look.

"All right! I fell asleep! But it was so boring! Why do I need to know what kind of gloves they wore in the fifteenth century?"

"Because you do, that's why. I want you to rewrite this book report by tomorrow! After you actually read the book!" Katarina shakes her finger at me. "You don't seem to appreciate the sacrifices I'm making for you. I'm sleeping in your jewelry box. I have to hide from your excruciatingly loud family. And your cat has tried to eat me fourteen times!"

Feeling guilty, I pick up the godmothering history book and say, "All right! All right! I *do* appreciate what you're doing for me. I'll finish this. I'm sure *you* read it cover to cover."

"Of course I did. I was an excellent student."

The old book shudders a little, and the pages flip back to Chapter One. I look at Katarina, annoyed. "You stopped at Chapter *One*?"

Katarina slams the book shut and shrugs. "I agree; it's a little dull. But until you get your client, that's all there is."

"When's that going to be? Me getting a client, I mean."

"I keep telling you, it's up to the godmothers. It could be next month, or there could be a messenger at the door right now."

There's a loud knock at my closed bedroom door. I gawk at it in surprise.

Katarina snaps, "Well, answer it!"

I go to the door, a little excited. I hope I get to help somebody nice, somebody who really needs me.

But it's not a messenger standing on the other side of the door; it's my sister, Madison. She's wearing one of her many, many pink tutus and has a feather in her hair. "Ta-da! We're twins!"

"We who?"

Then I hear a small, sad meow.

I glance down and see my unhappy-looking orange cat, Julius, sitting at Madison's feet. He's also wearing a pink tutu, and Madison has Scotch-taped a feather to his head. "Madison! You're humiliating him!"

"He looks beautiful."

"He looks stupid!" I pick him up and hold him in my lap. "You can't play with him like this. He's not your cat."

"But *you* never play with him anymore."

I hate it when my five-year-old sister is right. Julius hasn't been able to come into my room in weeks, because whenever he does, he tries to eat Katarina. (She's the best kitty treat he's ever had.)

I tell Madison, "Well, I'm going to play with him now."

I close the door and sit on my bed with Julius in my arms. He purrs—and then he stiffens and makes a chirping sound. He's spotted Katarina on my dresser; it's all I can do to hold on to him.

Katarina points at the door. "That beast has to go!"

"But I miss him! And it's his room, too."

"Not anymore. Evict him!"

I can't evict Julius; instead, I have a brilliant idea. I pull my magic wand out of my pocket. It's about the size of a pin (usually they shrink the fairy to match the wand, but I've been able to avoid that so far).

"What do you think you're doing?" Katarina asks.

"Fixing our Julius problem." I raise the wand and chant, "This room is more bearable, when Katarina tastes terrible." But I don't toss the spell at Julius—I toss it at Katarina.

Katarina's eyes cross when the spell hits her, and then they uncross and glare at me. "Lacey, you've entirely violated the student-teacher relationship. You are dis—"

Before I can stop him, Julius leaps away from me and half-swallows Katarina, whose little feet kick wildly. Since her head is in Julius's throat, I can't hear the rest of what she's hollering. Was she about to say: *You are disgusting, disobedient, disappointing,* or some other *dis* word entirely?

A second later Julius spits Katarina out. She lands on the dresser, her glasses askew and her hair dripping with cat spit. Shaking his head like he's just tasted a rotten lemon, Julius gives Katarina one more sniff, and then, revolted, he jumps off the dresser onto the bed next to me.

Katarina straightens her glasses and finally finishes the sentence she started: "You are disgraceful!"

Disgraceful! A *dis* word I didn't even think of. "Maybe I'm disgraceful, but my spell worked!"

Julius curls up on the bed and goes to sleep. He's obviously decided that rotten-lemon-flavored fairies aren't worth the trouble.

Katarina pulls a little brush out of my jewelry box and yanks it through her hair to get out the drool. "Fine! The fleabag can stay! Have fun setting your alarm clock for 12:01."

"For 12:01?"

"You should know by now that every fairy godmother spell ends at midnight. And I refuse to be eaten by a cat while I'm sleeping—it's so discombobulating!" (Another *dis* word!) "So you'll have to recast your spell at 12:01."

"Every day?"

"Consider it homework."

Katarina crawls into the little jewelry box she uses as a bed. She mutters to herself, "I don't taste terrible! Fairies taste delicious." Then she licks her arm and shudders. "Ew. I *do* taste terrible!" The jewelry box snaps closed.

I sigh and set my alarm clock for 12:01. Now I even have homework in the middle of the night.

CHAPTER 2

I rush into homeroom just as the first bell rings. Katarina used to come to school in my pocket, but she stopped doing that weeks ago. She told me, "As long as you don't have a client, I might as well stay home and enjoy my miserable new life." (Katarina's exact words.)

My best friend, Sunny Varden, leans over as I slide into my chair. "Why are you late?"

"I'm not late!" I snap.

"Okay, you're not late. Why are you crabby?" Sunny knows me better than anybody.

"Sorry. I had to get up at midnight to do a magic spell, and then I couldn't go back to sleep."

"Fun magic or homeschool magic?"

"Homeschool magic."

Sunny gives me a sympathetic smile. "Katarina's *tough*."

There are only a few people who know about me and Katarina, and Sunny is one of them. Another is Paige Harrington, who was my first fairy godmother client and is now my other best friend.

Oh, there *is* one more person who knows about me and Katarina: the school's former principal. But after I helped Principal Nazarino have her dream wedding with the basketball coach, they went to Hawaii for their honeymoon and decided to stay there forever. So now we have Principal Conehurst . . . whose voice suddenly blares out of the TV screen at the front of the classroom, which is showing a picture of the flag on the school's front lawn.

"Good morning, Lincoln Middle School! Please rise for the Pledge of Allegiance."

We used to do the pledge with no help from the television. But Principal Conehurst likes the morning webcast. It's sort of a fake news program, just for the school. If Principal Conehurst was the only one doing the webcast, it wouldn't be so bad. He's got a low, rumbly voice that's easy to ignore.

But after the pledge, the screen cuts to the school "newsroom," which is actually a table in the library. Makayla Brandice, my least-favorite cheerleader, sits at a microphone pretending to be a newscaster and loving every second of it. "Good morning, Lincoln! This is Makayla Brandice, your eyes and ears on the school." Now *there's* a voice that's not easy to ignore. She's done so many cheers that her volume is set at extra loud and extra-extra irritating. "Today's lunch menu is pasta with meat sauce and cheesy breadsticks. The side dishes are green beans and applesauce. Give me a Y-U-M for YUM!"

I put my head on my desk and moan. "Wake me when sixth grade is over."

Sunny pats my arm and says, "Let's go to the mall after school. That'll make you feel better."

"I can't. Katarina says I can only miss magic homeschooling if I have something for real school."

Sunny frowns. "Magic is cool—but that means you're going to school twice every day. Once is hard enough."

"I agree a million percent."

On the screen, Makayla shuffles through her papers. "And don't forget to be a Lincolnite!"

"What's a Lincolnite?" I ask Sunny.

"It's Principal Conehurst's new name for all the after-school clubs."

"Can't we just call them *after-school clubs*?"

Sunny shrugs. "*Lincolnite* is fancier."

Makayla talks a little louder on the TV, almost as if she can hear us interrupting her. "This afternoon is Lincolnite sign-up day in the school parking lot! There's a club for everyone, even if you're a total loser!" She smiles at the camera like she's just said something really sweet and thoughtful.

Sunny turns to me and says, "Lacey! You should sign up for some clubs!"

"I don't have time to join a club. I barely have time to eat."

"Think about it. Katarina says you can skip magic home-schooling if you have something for school—and the clubs are a part of school."

I *do* think about it. On the one hand, joining a bunch of clubs would give me more work to do. On the other hand, every time I'm at a club meeting, I won't be with Katarina.

It's a no-brainer! "Sunny, you're a genius! I'll text Paige, too."

After our last classes, Sunny, Paige, and I meet at the edge of the school parking lot. Paige's blond hair shines in the sun—she's the prettiest girl I know. And even though she's head cheerleader, she's also really nice. At our school, at least, nice and cheerleader don't usually go together. (See: Makayla.)

A long, long row of folding tables has been set up in the middle of the parking lot, with a huge sign in front: WELCOME LINCOLNITES!

There are tables for the French Club, the Spanish Club, the Practical Jokers Society, the Science Club, Craft-N-Crunch, the Anime-Maniacs, the Weightlifting Club, Speedcubing, the Toast Club (which isn't about making speeches; it's really about making the jam-and-butter kind), the Drama Club, the

Uni-Cyclones, the History Club, Origami for World Peace, and Soccer Boot Camp. There's even a table for the school webcast, where admiring kids cluster around Makayla like she's a celebrity. Makayla was popular before the morning show—now she's a TV star, or at least a webcast star.

"How many clubs do you want to join?" Paige asks me.

"One for every day of the week."

Paige looks surprised. "Seriously?"

"Any club would be better than being home with Katarina."

"I hear Makayla needs an assistant for the webcast," Paige says, trying not to smile.

"Correction: *almost* any club would be better than Katarina."

As we all walk along the tables, we decide to join a club together. Unlike me, Sunny and Paige only want to join one. (*They're* not trying to get out of fairy godmother homeschooling.) We eventually decide to sign up for Craft-N-Crunch, which is run by Mrs. Fleecy, the school secretary. Mrs. Fleecy's plan is for us to make jewelry (the craft part) and eat Rice Krispies treats (the crunch part). We like this plan.

"One club down, four to go!" I say.

Then we stop in front of the table for the Boy with the Longest Eyelashes in the World Club. (Joking!) It's actually the table where Scott Dearden, the cutest boy in school, is signing up people for the Uni-Cyclones while riding a unicycle backward. He's *that* talented.

"Hi, Lacey!" Scott calls out to me. "You're signing up, right? We'll have fun!"

Sunny smiles, Paige nudges me, and I turn bright red. I have to say right here: Scott is not my boyfriend. We're just friends.

"Gee, Scott, I don't think I'm coordinated enough for a unicycle."

"If you can ride a bike, you can ride one of these! I'm a good teacher."

"But I don't *have* a unicycle."

"You can buy one really cheap online."

I hesitate and then sign his list. Maybe I'll get killed, but unicycles do look like fun. Plus I'll get to spend time with Scott. Don't tell Sunny and Paige I said that.

A couple of minutes later, I also sign up for the French Club (*ooh la la!*) and the Donate a Sheep Club (*ewe la la!*), and I just need one more to fill out my schedule.

We walk up to a table that has an enormous sign made out of aluminum foil: FUTURE FLYERS. The kid at the table, Martin Shembly, sees us and waves excitedly. "Hi, guys! You're just in time for the demonstration!"

Paige, Sunny, and I haven't known Martin very long. What I mainly know is that he's really brainy. He plays the violin and is both a Trekkie and a Lord of the Rings fanatic. He's also funny and, beneath his thick glasses, sort of cute.

Martin and Sunny have been hanging out some while I've

been busy with homeschooling. They watch the super duper extended versions of the Lord of the Rings movies at Sunny's house, and I know she kind of likes him. But that's all I know, because I've been a horrible friend lately.

Usually, when you're best friends with someone, you know every detail about what's going on with them. But *usually* you don't have a three-inch-tall fairy living in your bedroom and taking up all your time.

We walk closer to Martin's table and see that he's holding a G.I. Joe doll (correction: *action figure*—boys get upset when you call them dolls) that has a little backpack strapped to its back. Maybe it's a parachute.

Sunny asks Martin, "Didn't your mom say you don't have time for a club?"

"What she doesn't know won't hurt her. This is going to be *maar*! That's Elvish for great and excellent!"

Just when I thought Martin couldn't get any more unusual, he starts talking Elf! No wonder people think he's a little strange.

"What's the club about?" Paige asks.

"We're going to build a real, working, low-cost jetpack! I've got the plans all drawn up—I just need six club members with leaf blowers," Martin explains. "And by the end of the month, we'll be flying!"

Sunny picks up the clipboard with the sign-up sheet. "How many people do you have so far?"

"Well, *no one*. That's why I'm doing this demonstration." Martin picks up a bullhorn and turns it on, sending out an ear-shattering screech of feedback. Kids all around us look at him and cover their ears. "Everybody! Prepare to be amazed!"

He holds the G.I. Joe figure in the air. "By the end of the month, my goal is to make a working, full-size version of *this*!" The kids watch, curious, as he pushes a button on G.I. Joe's backpack.

But Joe doesn't fly—he just makes a really, really, *really* loud farting noise: *POOOT!*

Every kid in the parking lot laughs. I do, too. I can't help myself—farts are funny. But when Martin turns bright red and looks miserable, I feel guilty.

When the laughter finally dies down (it takes a long time), Sunny tells Martin, "It almost worked. And nobody thought *you* made the sound."

At the edge of the parking lot, Makayla peers into her cell phone camera and says, loudly, "This is Makayla Brandice, your eyes and ears of the school. And *that* was a demonstration of a so-called jetpack."

The phone of almost every kid in the parking lot—including mine—buzzes with a school webcast alert. I look at it and see that Makayla has uploaded a video with the heading "Fartin' Martin." It already has over two hundred clicks, and the numbers are going up every second.

Martin looks away from his own phone, straightens his shoulders, and says, "Onward! Every great invention has a few bumps along the way." He turns to me, Sunny, and Paige hopefully. "You guys are signing up, right? The club meets Thursdays."

Sunny, Paige, and I all look at each other. We like Martin, but that's when Craft-N-Crunch meets. Future flying just can't compete with jewelry and Rice Krispies.

"We can't," I say. "We already signed up with Mrs. Fleecy."

Sunny tells him, "But don't worry! A lot of kids are going to think your club is really great. You won't even miss us."

Then there's another fart from G.I. Joe.